WITHDRAWN

Last Door to Aiya

Last Door

A Selection of
the Best New Science Fiction from
the Soviet Union

EDITED AND TRANSLATED BY

Mirra Ginsburg

to Aiya

S. G. PHILLIPS   *New York*

Contents

EDITOR'S INTRODUCTION

Imagination speaks a universal language. In modern industrial society this language makes use of the facts and concepts of our time. The world within and the world without, time and space and energy, harnessed or still untamed, hold the attention of science fiction writers everywhere, in Soviet Russia as well as in the United States.

In recent years there has been a particular upsurge in the field of science fiction in Russia. Contributors include doctors, physicists, mathematicians, astronomers, engineers and geologists, as well as linguists, journalists and writers. Sometimes working in collaboration, at other times independently, they have turned their minds and talents to the expanding limits of knowledge and ventured beyond them to speculate on what is still to come. These are not hack writers, piling up shock for mere horror's sake or resorting to gimmicks when the imagination fails. At their best, their works are richly inventive, witty, original and skillfully written. Their themes range far and wide: space, time and timelessness; the relationship between man and machine; the present and the future (or the past, as in "Homer's Secret"); earth creatures versus beings from other planets, as in "Out in Space" or in the magnificent, warm and terrifying story, "Last Door to Aiya"; dehumanized men, humanized machines, and even strange phenomena within the human psyche itself, as in "The New Signal Station." Often, as in "The World in Which I Disappeared" and "My Colleague," the fantasy is mingled with humor to delightful effect. Frequently, as in "The Golden Lotus" and the moving and poetic story "The White Cone of the Alaid," the author deals with man's unconquerable, questing spirit.

This collection is a sampling of what is being done in Russia today by some of the finest Soviet science fiction writers. The stories, all of them recent, have appeared in the original Russian within the past ten years.

Last Door to Aiya

1

The World in Which I Disappeared

By A. DNEPROV

I was sold and brought to Woodrop's house from the morgue. There is nothing strange about this, just as there is nothing strange about my being in the morgue. The simple fact was that I had slashed my veins in my bathroom in the New World Hotel. Were it not for the money I owed the hotel, I would not have been found so soon. Or, rather, I would have been found too late. But I owed a great deal, and it was partly because of my debts that I made the abortive attempt to move on to a better world. I was also most impatient to meet my improvident parents and tell them what I thought of them and, generally, of people who breed children for our civilized society.

As I know today, Woodrop bought me for eighteen dollars and nine cents. Of this sum, three dollars and nine cents were paid for the blanket in which he had wrapped me. So that my net value is fifteen dollars. This is the standard price for a homeless cadaver bought for medical experiments. I am homeless enough to fit into this category. However, there is one point, it seems to me, that the law did not adequately provide for. I think it is unwise to sell cadavers for medical experiments before they have been cooled off for a sufficient period in the refrigerators.

I can imagine the speed at which Woodrop drove me from the morgue to his cottage in Green Valley! If it were not for this speed, his money would have gone down the drain.

Instead of me, he would have gotten a shabby old blanket, plus the expense of my funeral.

I was revived according to every proper rule of procedure. They gave me a transfusion of three liters of blood and an adrenalin injection, pumped glucose with cod liver oil into me, wrapped me around with a tangle of electric wires and heaters. After a while Woodrop switched off the current. I began to breathe without outside help, and my heart began to beat as though I had never died.

I opened my eyes and saw Woodrop and a young woman.

"How do you feel?" asked Woodrop, a character in a white coat, with the face of man whose hobby was slaughtering cattle.

"Thank you, sir. Very well, sir. Who are you, sir?"

"I am not a sir. I am Woodrop, Harry Woodrop, Doctor of Medicine and Sociology, Honorary Member of the Institute of Radio-Electronics," Harry growled. "Are you hungry?"

I nodded.

"Bring him a plate of soup."

The girl slipped off her chair and disappeared. Harry Woodrop pulled up my shirt without a by-your-leave and injected some chemical into me.

"Now you're completely alive," he said.

"Yes, sir."

"Harry Woodrop."

"Yes, sir, Harry Woodrop."

"I hope your intellectual capacities are not too well developed?"

"I hope not."

"Your education?"

"Almost none. I graduated from some sort of a university. But that doesn't mean a thing."

I had decided to myself that Harry would have least need for people with higher education.

"Hm . . . What did you learn there?"

It seemed to me that I'd do best to disclaim any knowledge.

"Golf, dancing, fishing, running after girls."

"Good. But don't try to apply your skills to Susan."

"Who is that?"

"The girl who went to get your supper."

"It is night already?"

"No, it's already the day before yesterday. And generally, you ask too many questions."

I decided that an ex-corpse should not ask too many questions of Harry Woodrop, M.D., Ph.D., and Honorary Member of the Institute of Radio-Electronics.

The next day, Susan said, "You will take part in the Eldorado Project. By the way, what's your name?"

"Harry."

"That's bad. The boss does not like any other Harrys around. You're not mistaken? It happens after death."

"No. And what is the Eldorado?" I asked.

"It is a world of happiness, prosperity, and social equilibrium. A world without Communists and unemployment."

"You rattle it off like a TV announcer."

"You have an important role in Eldorado."

"Really? What role?"

"You'll be the working class."

"What? Who?"

"Not who, but what. The proletariat."

I thought for a moment, and asked: "Are you sure I was brought back to life?"

"Quite sure."

"And what will be your role in Eldorado?"

"I will be the 'manufacturers' association.' "

Susan went out, and Harry Woodrop came in.

"From now on we shall not feed you."

13

"Excellent! Are you studying the process of death from starvation?" I asked.

"A stale joke!"

"All the same, what will I eat?"

"You'll have to go to work."

"Do you still have the blanket so I can be taken back?"

"In my highly organized society, finding you work won't be any problem."

"I will have to do a lot of tramping and looking. I won't be able to take it."

"You won't have to go anywhere."

"How then?"

"You will merely have to press a button. When you're hired, you will get wages. And once there are wages, there will be food."

"Take me to that button, quick!"

"Your psychological factor isn't quite ready yet. You will not be able to press the button with sufficient enthusiasm."

"I'll press it with any kind of enthusiasm you say!"

"In the interest of the experiment, you'll have to go hungry for another hour or two."

"I'll complain!"

"You will not complain, because you do not exist."

"How's that?"

"You are long dead."

The Eldorado consisted of three huge machines standing in different corners of a spacious hall. They were connected by wires and cables. One machine stood behind a glass partition. Harry Woodrop sat down in front of the control panel in the center of the hall and said:

"Schizophrenics, professors, and senators are trying to improve our society with the aid of committees and subcommittees, foundations, voluntary commissions, economic conferences, and ministries of social welfare. Nonsense! All it

14

takes is four hundred and two triodes, one thousand, five hundred and seventy-five resistors, and two thousand, four hundred and ninety-one condensers, and the whole problem is solved. This is the diagram of our social organization for today."

Harry Woodrop unrolled a blueprint with a diagram.

"On the right is the 'production' block; on the left, the 'consumption' block. Between them we have positive and negative feedback. By switching around the radio tubes and other parts of our 'society,' we can find a way of keeping the system from slipping into either the state of hyperregeneration or that of damped oscillations. When I achieve this, the problem will be solved once and for all!"

As he explained his brilliant plan, Harry Woodrop waved his arms and swiveled his head in all directions. It must have been a habit of his.

"But I have taken care of something even more important," he went on. "I brought the human element into the scheme. And since it would be both irrational and too expensive to replace it by an equivalent electronic robot with a limited memory, this will be your function," Harry pointed at me, "and yours," he said, turning to Susan.

Then he clasped his hands beind his back and walked around the control box four times.

"Here," he banged his fist on the lid of the box, "is the brain of our 'society'—its 'government.' The neon light above performs the function of a president; in other words, it stabilizes the tension. So!"

Susan and I looked tenderly at the "president," who glowed with a rosy light.

"And now to work! You—off to 'production'! And you—to 'consumption.' "

An original case of electronic modeling fever, I thought. At the university, the professors used to say that with the help of radio electronics you can build any models you wish: turtles, lathes, interplanetary ships, and even a model of man. Harry Woodrop built an electronic model of our state. And he not only built it, but decided to perfect it, to develop a harmonious structure for it. It will be interesting to see how far he gets with it.

I went to the machine on the right. Susan disappeared behind the glass screen, in the "consumption" sphere.

"What must I do?" I asked.

"What you did in life. Work."

"Excellent advice! I am as hungry as a hyena!"

"First you must get work in the 'production sphere.' "

"How?"

"Press the white button on the right."

"What is she going to do?" I nodded in Susan's direction.

"What business does."

I sat motionless before the huge metal case. Its front panel glittered with dials; multicolored buttons, switches, and levers projected from it everywhere. In this machine, Harry embodied the economic and political structure of the world we live in. Material goods were created here in the form of electric energy which circulated along the leads between the "production sphere" and the "consumption sphere."

I pressed the white button.

"Your occupation?" the machine barked.

O-ho, just as in real life! The machine is even interested in my occupation! I thought, and answered: "Artist. . . ."

"We don't need any."

I looked questioningly at Woodrop.

"Shall I press the white button too?" asked Susan.

"Of course."

"And what will happen?"

"You will receive the surplus value accumulated in the scheme."

16

Susan's relay clicked.

I pressed the white button again.

"Occupation?"

"Dentist."

"Don't need any."

Susan pressed her button again, and a dress slid out of the automat.

I was still desperately trying to get work.

"Occupation?" the machine repeated stupidly.

"Mechanic."

"Come back in a month."

The electronic model of production functioned perfectly. How many times, before I found myself with Woodrop, had I gone out to look for work and heard exactly the same questions and the same answers!

"It won't work, boss," I turned to Woodrop.

"Don't look, I want to put on my new dress," cried Susan.

"Boss, I cannot wait a month!"

"Try again. I've reduced the negative grid bias of the 'labor-wanted' transmitting tube."

Susan pressed her button but the machine gave her nothing.

"What's wrong?" she protested.

Harry nodded at me: "When he creates 'surplus value' your automat will switch on again. We have now come to the 'capital accumulation' phase."

I pressed the white button.

"Occupation?"

"Stevedore."

"Hired!"

A lever jumped out of the machine and almost hit me in the stomach.

"Work!" shouted Harry from his control panel.

"How?"

17

"Pump the lever up and down."

I began to pump the lever. It moved very stiffly.

"How long do I have to do this?"

"Until you get your wages."

"And how will that happen?"

"Tokens will drop into the box under your nose. You can use them to eat, drink, and amuse yourself."

I pumped the lever up and down until my arm ached. I stopped for a moment.

"What are you doing?" shouted Harry.

"I want to take a rest."

"You'll be fired!"

I seized the lever and frantically began to make up for lost time.

I tried to visualize the electronic block that could "fire" me. By moving the lever, I thought, I must be creating electrical charges which were relayed to the block and kept it in working condition. By stopping, I would bring into action the mechanism that withdrew the lever inside the case.

"Ah, my automat is working again!" cried Susan.

Perspiration dripped from my forehead.

"When do I get my wages, boss?"

Woodrop was busy with the "president." Without looking at me, he muttered:

"I'm watching the apparatus. There must be maximum profits."

"When do I get my tokens?" I repeated.

"When the anode voltage you create in the condenser unlocks the thyratron."

"I'm hungry. . . ."

"You work badly. Every swing of the lever produces only one and a half volts. Pump faster."

Susan switched on her automat again. She received a second dress.

"I don't want any more dresses," she said.

"What do you want?"

"What you promised. A coat."

"In a moment I'll add more negative bias to the grid and shift some voltage from his condenser to your automat."

I knew it! In Woodrop's scheme, the role of capital was played by electric energy. And he was drawing this energy away from my 'production sphere' to the 'consumption sphere,' into the pockets of the 'manufacturers' association.' The models of the pockets were the condensers and accumulators.

"That's too much! Why the devil must she get everything?"

The automat clicked. Tokens dropped, rattling, into the drawer in front of my sweating nose.

"Collect your wages."

I gathered five copper tokens.

"What am I to do with them?"

"Go to the 'consumption sphere' and use the automat."

I ran behind the screen.

"Ah, corpse!" Susan cried gaily. "You have to use this automat next to mine."

I received a bowl of soup, a cold meatball, and a mug of beer. Thank God for that!

My first working day was over. Susan went to bed, taking along her dresses.

I wondered what would happen the next day!

When I arrived at the "production sphere" on the following morning my lever was not there. Susan sat in an armchair next to the "president," drinking beer.

"What's the matter?" I wondered out loud.

"You've been fired," she said, grinning, and nodded at the clock on the wall. It was five minutes past eight.

"Why was I fired?"

19

"For lateness. Try to get work again."

"Where did you get the beer?"

"I used your tokens. They are mine now."

I had never seen such brazenness before!

I pressed the white button.

"Occupation?" asked the machine.

"Stevedore," I replied without thinking.

"Unfavorable references," said the machine and was silent.

The machine, it turned out, possessed a memory! It took note of my dismissal for lateness. Again, everything was just as in real life. Perhaps these electronic models of economic and social structures really did make sense? And yet, I could not believe that such an extremely complex phenomenon as the social life of many millions of living human beings could be expressed with sufficient exactness in terms of radio tubes, transistors, resistors and relays.

I wondered what to do next. My eyes fell on the electronic brain. If it controlled the whole electronic model, why not try to improve it in my own way?

"You're not a tattletale, are you?" I asked Susan.

"Why?"

"I want to try and improve 'society.' "

"Go ahead."

I went over to the control board and pulled a handle at random. Then another, and a third. There were dozens of them. The machine roared madly. The "president," who had emitted a faint glow until then, flared up like a wax candle. In the hope of making my lever come out again, I pulled the "president" out of his socket and hid him in my pocket. At that moment Woodrop entered.

"Ah, a mutiny! That's good! An attempt against the government? Marvelous! And where is the voltage equalizer? Liquidation of the supreme authority? Excellent! Return the 'president,' if you please."

I returned the neon tube.

"We shall provide for this human element, too. I shall screen off the 'government' and protect it with a high voltage line. Two thousand volts will do. We shall put the 'president' under a bell and protect him with a five-thousand volt line. This way. Now the 'government' will be secure against domestic disorders."

I was totally annihilated. Harry Woodrop connected high-tension lines to the electronic brain.

"Give me any kind of work," I pleaded.

"Try again now, before I restore all the potentiometers to their previous positions."

I pressed the "labor-wanted" button. The loud speaker suddenly sang out in the voice of a well-known radio star, "How happily you died in my pale-blue embrace. . . ." Not one, but three levers came out all at once from the machine and began to rock up and down without any external help. Tokens poured into the drawer as from a horn of plenty!

"What luck, boss! I think we're really getting to Eldorado!" I exclaimed, gathering up the copper discs.

"Like hell," Harry grunted. "There is nothing in the 'consumption sphere.' It's empty."

I rushed behind the partition and slipped a token into the automat. No reaction. Silence.

"Mm—yes. Production has simply gone crazy."

Harry Woodrop's electronics evidently functioned only in a strictly delimited manner. The "production" and "consumption" models balanced themselves at a point of unstable equilibrium. The moment the machine's regime was disturbed, it went berserk. It turned into a senseless cluster of radio schemes which worked without rhyme or reason.

Harry set the potentiometers and all the levers but one disappeared into the machine. The tenor changed to a contralto,

21

then to a coloratura soprano, and fell silent on a "mi." I seized the remaining lever and energetically began to pump it to re-establish my reputation.

"Give me back the tokens," said Harry.

"Why?"

"You got them for nothing. That's improper."

"And why does she get everything for nothing?" I pointed at Susan, who had fallen asleep in the armchair.

"Don't ask stupid questions and give me the tokens."

Nevertheless, I managed to secrete two tokens.

Susan slept through the entire working day but by evening I had earned another seven tokens. Woodrop in the meantime had secured the "government" from further attack and had twice drawn away the energy from my condenser. Generally, he fussed over his machine with great zeal. Afterward, Susan told me that Harry had gotten a large grant for his Eldorado Project.

Now I was more prudent and spent only two tokens for food. It left me half-hungry but I realized that I had to think of a rainy day.

Next morning I found Susan red-eyed.

"What's the 'manufacturers' association' bawling about?" I asked maliciously.

I had come to work early. The clinking of tokens in my pockets put me in a good mood.

"Disgusting!" said Susan.

"What?"

"He took everything away. The dress, the undies, the coat."

"Who?"

"Woodrop."

"Why?"

"To start everything from the beginning. He put them back in the automat."

I left my lever and went over to Susan. I felt sorry for her.

22

"I don't think I like this game very much," I said.

"I don't like it either any more."

"It's all right. Harry will manage to establish harmony."

"I don't know what this means. All I know is that it's disgusting—taking away what was given to you."

Woodrop entered.

"What are you up to there? Back to your places! I must have set the thyratron potential too high. You're loafing, and you were not fired."

"One second, boss!"

I ran to my lever but it was too late. It was gone. Woodrop grinned, delighted.

To hell with you, I thought. I have enough tokens for today. Susan sulked and no longer used her automat. I reluctantly pressed the white button, naming various occupations. None were needed. Could our "society" have reached the saturation point in its supply of doctors, teachers, technicians, cooks? I pressed the white button again.

"Occupation?"

"Journalist."

"Hired."

I was stunned. A desk with a typewriter emerged from the machine. That Harry! He had thought of everything!

"The press is a profitable business in our 'society,' " said Woodrop. "Your earnings will depend on your popularity. The more Susan enjoys your compositions, the more you will get. You can start right now."

Woodrop went out.

I sat down at the typewriter and began to think. Then I wrote:

Extra! Extra! Colossal, sensational! New animals appear as a result of radioactive mutations! Talking asses! Dog mathematicians! Ape homeopaths! Singing pigs! Poker-playing roosters!

"What trash," said Susan, pulling a sheet of paper from her automat. "If this goes on, I will not read, and you will die of hunger."

"You don't like it?" I asked.

"No."

"All right, I'll try something else."

Colossal, sensational! Eighteen billionnaires and forty-two millionnaires turn over their billions and millions to the workers. . . .

"Listen, Sam, or whatever your name is! I won't read your ridiculous nonsense any more."

"Give me another chance."

"I won't."

"Please, Susan!"

"I don't want to."

"Oh, Susie!"

"Don't dare to call me Susie!"

I typed:

Susie, you are a wonderful girl. I love you.

She said nothing.

I love you. Are you reading?

"Yes," she said quietly. "Go on."

I've loved you from the moment I revived. All the time we've been fussing with this idiotic project I've been thinking of how we can escape together. You and I. Do you want to?

"Yes," she replied quietly, pulling the sheet of paper from her automat.

I stopped typing and turned to her.

"This is what I've thought up. After all, I have a profession. We'll get away from Woodrop and try to find real work, not this electronic nonsense. It will be easier for us because we'll be together. Honestly, after I saw you I came to the conclusion that it's stupid to slash veins."

"I think so, too," whispered Susie.

Woodrop entered.

He looked at his apparatus and snapped his fingers.

"Ah! Things are moving, it seems to me. The tension is stabilized! No more phase displacements! We are approaching harmony between 'production' and 'consumption.' "

"Certainly, boss," I said. "Oour 'society' should start living decently some day, after all."

"Continue in the same spirit. I'll enter this in the diagram," he said and walked out.

"Let us meet here tonight. We'll jump out of the window."

"All right. . . ."

By the end of the day I had composed about ten idiotic reports and earned a pile of tokens. Susan pulled out sheet after sheet, demonstrating to the electronic blockhead her interest in my output. The harmony was complete, and Harry Woodrop feverishly traced the diagram of his Eldorado in order to sell it for a million dollars. It was well worth it, for it took full account of the human element!

I bought sandwiches with all my tokens and stuffed them into my pockets.

At night, tiptoeing to the window, Susan and I halted near the "manufacturers' association."

"You did not use your automat yesterday."

"If I had, you would have earned less."

"We can take the dresses and the coat, if you want them."

"To the devil with them!"

"I can leave a note saying that I did it. I don't exist, anyway."

"Who needs them? It will be easier to walk without packages."

We climbed out of the window, swung over the fence, and found ourselves on a wide asphalt road, leading to a big city. Over the city hung a frenzied, flaming orange sky. For a moment, Susan pressed herself to me.

"Don't be afraid. There are two of us now."

I put my arm around her and we marched forward. After a while, I stopped under a street light and, looking into the girl's trusting eyes, asked:

"Susie, how did you get to Woodrop?"

She smiled faintly, stretched her left arm and showed me her wrist. An elongated red scar stood out sharply on the white skin.

"You too?"

She nodded. And we went on, two people who do not exist. . . .

2

The New Signal Station

By S. GANSOVSKY

There must be something to it after all, although science has not yet learned to understand it. Yet, when I think of it, I am almost tempted to accuse myself of being mystical. But let's not try to label everything. Let's try, instead, to recall our own experiences—for example, at the front in wartime.

I remember one night at the Leningrad front in 1941, in early September, when my comrade and I were returning from reconnaissance. The Gulf of Finland was to the right of us, with Kronstadt somewhere in the dark, beyond the waves. To the left were the bushes and thickets of Peterhof Park. The entire territory was in our hands, since the front line was two miles to the left, beyond the railway line, and the park was filled with our units. We strode along without a care, and even slung our automatics behind our shoulders. Suddenly I sensed that we were about to be shot at. That very moment. The feeling was so strong that I shouted "Get down!" and, jumping on my comrade, knocked him to the ground. At once, a chain of tracer bullets like a line of glowing sparks flew silently across the darkness overhead, and a moment later, as if separately, came the burst of Tommy gun fire. Of course, we instantly opened fire at the bushes and later ran to the spot, but by then the enemy had disappeared.

What was it, though? *What* had told me that someone was aiming at us? Whence came this certainty, when we were walking through an area of complete quiet? But it did come, and if we had not thrown ourselves on the ground in time, the fire would surely have cut us down. In the morning we would have been found on the road, stiff and gray faced, and the fellows of the nearby Seventh Marine Brigade would have given us a thin rifle salute in parting and, scowling silently, would have buried us in a common grave. And I would not be here with you to remember anything today.

Or take another instance. In 1942, near Kalach, when we faced the Eighth Italian Army. . . .

But no. Let's not digress, but let me tell you what happened to Kolya Zvantsov. I heard the story from him in Leningrad in the winter of 1943, when we were both in the convalescent battalion on Zagorodny Prospect, in the large gray building across the way from the railroad station. As you know, a man was sent to the convalescent battalion from the hospital when he no longer needed hospital care but was not ready to return to military duty. Our wounds had not yet healed completely and needed bandaging. During the day all of us—except for those who were excused—had training, arms study and drill. And in the evening, lying on wooden bunks, we exchanged stories of things we had known, seen and heard. We heard tales of Uritsk, a suburb of Leningrad, which had changed hands six times in hand-to-hand fighting, of Volga crossings, of the battles under Mozdok, and so on. For some reason, we always spoke about the war. Perhaps because we ourselves were in the rear at the time. It's a well-known fact: in wartime, the front-line men seldom talk about battles when they have a moment's rest, but more about prewar life. But in hospitals and on leave, the front is always the main topic.

It was during our quiet evenings on Zagorodny that Nikolay Zvantsov told us what had happened to him. Or, rather, not "to him," but "through him." A strange power had manifested itself through him, had done its work, as it were, and disappeared.

It happened in May of 1942, during our advance on Kharkov from the Izyum salient. The operation, as you know, had not been sufficiently well prepared. The Germans counterattacked from the Slavyansk area. Many divisions of our Sixth, Ninth, and Fifty-seventh Armies were surrounded and fought desperately to break through the enemy lines and withdraw behind the Northern Donets.

Zvantsov served in a machine gun artillery battalion. At the end of May his company held its position for two weeks near a small village, the name of which he had forgotten. The situation was alarming. The sector occupied by the company was quiet but some large troop movements were taking place just ahead of it. Heavy shell fire was already heard from the flanks; it was known that the regiment next to ours had been driven back. There was growing danger of encirclement by the enemy, and orders were awaited from division headquarters, but liaison had broken down.

The surrounding areas became depopulated. The village where the company was stationed was virtually abandoned. It had received its first baptism of fire in 1941, when the Germans had taken Kharkov and the entire region was the site of major battles. And the few houses that had survived at that time were razed by the SS-men of the Fourth Tank Division as they retreated during our recent breakthrough to Merefa.

The village was thus no more than a waste of ruins, beginning to be overgrown here and there by sparse shrubs. The only building that still afforded shelter was a half-collapsed brick house, where the command personnel of the company was lodged. And the only two remaining residents of the village—an old man of sixty-five and his deaf-mute daughter—occupied the cellar. The old man shared his rather plentiful supply of potatoes, piled up in the cellar, with our

29

men. He also helped them, together with his daughter, to dig trenches and emplacements for the guns.

It was in that village that Nikolay began to experience a series of strange phenomena, which took the form of extraordinary dreams. But the first time his new powers manifested themselves was one morning, when the commander sent him out on reconnaissance.

Nikolay and another private, Abramov, went out to determine the enemy's exact location. They walked about five miles without encountering either Russian or German troops. Then, while lying on a hill beyond a small wood, they heard the sound of approaching tanks. Soon the tanks emerged from the wood. Zvantsov recognized one of our fast T-70s and two "thirty-fours." This might have been a tank reconnaissance unit, and Nikolay decided to wait until the tanks came nearer and then to halt them and ask about the general situation.

The two men lay quietly, waiting, when Zvantsov had a sudden feeling that they were not the only observers, that there were other eyes—and not one pair, but many—closely watching the tanks and calculating the distance as they approached. This feeling was so powerful that he turned his head and scanned the terrain; then he pointed to another wooded spot about two hundred yeards away. Both men peered closely and both caught sight at the same moment of the faint movement of a rising "snake"—a German antitank gun, given this nickname by our soldiers because of its long slender muzzle and the small head of its recoil brake.

At that instant the first well-aimed shot rang out and a shell whizzed through the air. The T-70 shook, its turret leaned over, and a huge cloud of black smoke burst from the tank. Nikolay Zvantsov felt almost physically the sudden incineration of three human bodies inside the tank in the heat and fury of exploding ammunition. In an instant all the thoughts, fears, courage, plans of those within were turned to ash, and three young Russians ceased to be.

Zvantsov and Abramov jumped up and shouted, as though their shouts could in some way help the men in the tanks, but then they recollected themselves and dropped down again to keep out of sight of the Germans.

In the meantime, the encounter gained momentum. The antitank battery which had lain in ambush in the woods opened a running fire against the two remaining tanks. The "thirty-fours" returned the fire and began to retreat.

And then Nikolay sensed once again that still another group of men was looking down from above—at them, at the battery, and at the tanks. He tugged Abramov's sleeve, and they rolled down the hillock into a ditch. And it was just in time, for a Junkers-88 passed at a low altitude directly over them, and a neat row of holes was traced in the sandy rim of the ditch, each with the glass drop at the center that forms when fast bullets from a large-caliber machine gun hit sand.

At the same moment, in some mysterious and incomprehensible fashion, Zvantsov was suddenly aware of the *total* picture of the encounter. He saw it in his mind as a huge polygon in space, with a moving angle at the summit—the roaring plane, and with many points on land: the German antitank battery, where the muzzles of the guns belched and swung over on the carriages; the clattering tanks, escaping from the fire; he himself, and Abramov; and, finally, a group of about a dozen tanks, silently hiding in a sparse wood in the distance, but already discovered by the Junkers-88. (He knew without a shadow of doubt that the tanks were there, although he could not understand why, how, and with what faculty he sensed it.)

The angles of the giant, shifting polygon were linked by a variety of relationships, and it was these relationships that somehow made it possible for Zvantsov to experience them. The artillery men of the Nazi battery wanted to destroy the "thirty-fours"; the tank crews strained to escape from the fire; the commander of the Junkers saw the tanks in the distant wood and intended to bomb them; and his machine gunner

31

regretted that he had not hit the two tiny figures at the edge of the wood, Zvantsov and Abramov. All these desires, intentions, and regrets passed through Zvantsov's consciousness and fused all that was happening into a single whole. It was as though he had acquired an additional internal organ of sight.

But that was not all.

He knew what was happening, but also for a brief moment he was able to foresee what was to come.

He knew beforehand that the two tanks would not turn in the direction of the copse from where they had come, but would go across the open field toward the distant wood. And indeed, no sooner did he sense it than the leading tank began to turn away from the trees.

Zvantsov knew that the Junkers would not pursue the two tanks, but would fly toward the wood; and, as if in obedience to his thought, the plane veered right, and only two seconds later swooped down in a dive over the distant wood.

He knew that the battery would now change its tactics, and before he had time fully to realize his knowledge, the "snakes" stopped their direct fire at the tanks and opened a ranging fire behind them.

For a few seconds, Zvantsov understood everything for everyone. He saw what could not be seen with the eyes; he read all the thoughts for miles around and felt not only the present but the immediate future.

Then all this ended, and he was himself again.

The tanks disappeared behind the hill, the battery was silent. The scouts crawled on their bellies to the copse and went to report the situation to their unit commander.

All that day Zvantsov wondered about the remarkable polygon and his sudden ability to see and feel what was inaccessible to either the eye or the senses.

After that came the dreams.

The first dream occurred that very evening, when he lay

down to sleep on the floor of the house where his company was lodged. The dream was extraordinarily vivid.

Zvantsov dreamed that he was in a wide, beautiful park like that in Gatchina near Leningrad, with huge century-old trees, sand-covered paths, and sumptuous flowerbeds. Beyond the lawn, on one side, he could see a two-story mansion, clean and well kept, and directly before him a small windowless lodge. Not even a lodge, but a marble-faced cube with a door in it. This lodge or cube was surrounded by a low, ornate wrought-iron fence.

When the dream began—and Zvantsov knew that this was a dream and not reality—he thought with some edge of his mind that he was in luck; he welcomed the opportunity to rest a while in such a beautiful park, if only in a dream. He needed a rest badly, for he had been at the front almost eleven months, retreating in battles from the very border; even during the regrouping of troops he had not halted anywhere for more than a week.

But very soon in the course of the dream he realized that he would have no rest, since everything went quite differently from what he would have wished.

He stood with his feet wide apart. From the distance came the roaring of a motor, and a large open truck loaded with shiny milk cans drove into the park. The truck stopped. Two men who had come in it sent the driver away and waited until he was gone. Then they hastily began to unload the heavy cans.

Zvantsov felt a bundle of keys in his hand. He opened the gate in the iron fence and then the door into the lodge. In the floor of the small windowless room there was a trap door, opening on a wide circular staircase. Zvantsov, followed by the men with the heavy cans, descended the staircase to another room, where five or six oak coffins stood on low supports.

What followed then was altogether inexplicable. Zvantsov and the men whom he was evidently directing began to remove the lids from the coffins, which were empty. One of the men opened the first milk can, and Zvantsov saw that, instead of milk, it contained parts of machine guns.

Zvantsov awakened with astonishment to see an unknown man in a large cap sitting on the floor two steps away from him and staring at him with wide-open, pale, greedy eyes.

For a moment or two they looked at each other, then the man in the cap turned away. Zvantsov was puzzled by the appearance of a stranger at company headquarters. In the rest of the room everything was in order. The gloomy Lieutenant Petrishchev, the company commander, was sitting in his usual place at the desk, bending over a map illuminated by a burning piece of German telephone wire. Abramov was sleeping on the only bed, lying on his back, his arms flung out and his mouth wide open. All the other men at the headquarters were also asleep, and through the window Zvantsov saw the starry sky and the dark figure of the sentry, resting on his rifle.

Zvantsov turned on his other side, closed his eyes, and immediately went on with his dream, but as though after an interruption.

Now he was in the mansion. He knew it because he was standing in a room and saw the same garden, with its avenues and flowerbeds, from the window. Next to Zvantsov was a gray-haired gentleman in a green jacket, riding breeches, and high, laced boots (in his dream, Zvantsov described this man to himself precisely as a "gentleman," not as a "man"). Zvantsov and the gentleman conversed in a foreign tongue. As a character in the dream, Zvantsov knew this language; as himself, Private Zvantsov, who was sleeping at the moment and aware that he was sleeping, he did not understand a word.

They spoke excitedly, gesturing with their hands. The gray-haired gentleman turned to the door and shouted something. The door opened at once, and two men brought in a third, who turned out to be the driver who had brought the truck into the garden in the earlier dream. He looked thinner now, with a hounded face and a torn lip. The old gentleman and Zvantsov—again as the hero of this strange dream— threw themselves upon the driver and began to beat him. At first he did not defend himself but merely covered his head. Then suddenly a knife flashed in his hand, he rushed forward and struck Zvantsov in the face. The knife slipped over his chin and grazed his neck. Then the others knocked the driver off his feet, and Zvantsov, pressing his hand over his neck, stepped aside, took a small mirror from his pocket, and looked.

In the mirror he saw another face, not his own. It was astonishing. Zvantsov was dreaming; he was the character in this dream, acted in it and was conscious of his "I." But when he looked into the mirror, the face was not his but someone else's. . . .

Zvantsov felt that somebody was shaking him and he woke up.

It was his turn for sentry duty outside the headquarters. He rose, took his semiautomatic, and went out swaying with fatigue into the street. He took up his post, feeling regretfully that the early morning breeze was blowing away the last bits of warmth from under his blouse.

He scanned the village, over which the dawn was beginning to rise and suddenly knew that he had seen the face that looked out at him from the mirror somewhere before. He had seen it quite recently, in fact. Perhaps a month ago, or a week, or even a day. At the same time, as often happens with dreams, he could not recollect the face itself.

The company spent the next twenty-four hours in a state of tension. Contact was re-established briefly with division headquarters, which ordered that the village be held at any cost, to assure the retreat of other large units. But the enemy did not show himself, and even the battery discovered by the scouts had withdrawn somewhere.

Since the night when Zvantsov had had his first dream, individual men began to straggle into the company's sector. They were soldiers of the infantry division which had received the first German tank thrust at Merefa, refused to retreat, and was almost totally annihilated, together with commander and staff. The glum Lieutenant Petrishchev directed the wounded farther back to the battalion; the able-bodied were retained to reinforce our defense.

It was on that same night, as Zvantsov learned later, that the stranger in the cap had wandered in. He was an odd fellow, a deputy of the division's Special Intelligence Section. His section had stumbled upon an SS tank division ambush early in May and lost three-quarters of its personnel. Udubchenko, as the stranger called himself, had served as an orderly with the section chief; after the catastrophe, he said, he had been promoted at once to deputy. Three days later his division was slashed to pieces, the section came under heavy bombardment, and he was the sole survivor. He had taken with him the remaining property of the section—a huge and very awkward Underwood typewriter and the only folder with documents that had not been destroyed—and began to make his way east, to our side.

Until his identity was verified, Petrishchev left him at headquarters. Udubchenko was evidently very anxious to be an intelligence man instead of being transferred to the ranks. He did not part with his file by day or by night. The company men kidded him, asking whether he would fight the Germans with his Underwood if the occasion arose. He replied that he had a TT revolver, and showed it.

Udubchenko seemed to have some special interest in Zvantsov. Nikolay noticed that he was always trying to remain alone with him, and when they worked together at digging trenches, he repeatedly caught the man's intent, greedy eyes upon him.

The next two days were fairly quiet. Platoon commanders and men were digging spare trenches and communication paths and worked out the firing sectors for machine guns. But the enemy seemed to have decided to leave the battalion alone. The clatter of artillery fire moved eastward. German U-52 transport planes passed over the battalion positions by day and night, holding the course of Izyum.

And again Zvantsov began to dream.

He dreamed that he was walking through a field of sunflowers. It was a dark night, but he walked confidently and came out to a wood. At the edge of the wood, over an old, half-collapsed trench, leaned a burned-out twin-turreted Soviet training tank, a veteran of the battles of 1941. Its armor was bloated from within, evidently pushed out by an explosion. And across the bulging wall, someone's hand had written with white paint in crude and illiterate Russian, *The armar is strong, and our tanks are fasst.* Zvanstov recognized the words, but was not angry and even smiled. However, from there on, he no longer strode freely, but bent down and began to run from tree to tree with light, catlike steps. He went on in this way for about half a mile, then flattened himself on the grass and crawled forward, until he came to a clearing, bright with moonlight. Zvantsov saw the silhouettes of some huge vehicles with covered tops and men in black coats, standing and walking near the vehicles. For a long time, Zvantsov watched them, then nodded with satisfaction and began to crawl back. . . .

Here the dream broke off. For a time, disconnected fragments of the first dream—in the park—flashed before him. Then came a new and long installment, without breaks.

Now Zvantsov was again standing at night in a large

deserted clearing in the woods, waiting for something and peering tensely at the sky. At last the sound of a plane came from the distance. Zvantsov took a flashlight from his pocket and signaled several times. The invisible plane came nearer, then withdrew. Zvantsov was not worried about it. He lay down on the grass and began to wait.

Some time later, a light flashed overhead at a great altitude, this time unaccompanied by the sound of motors. Zvantsov immediately took from his pocket a second flashlight and signaled with both. The light began to drop precipitously, then went out. A huge dark bird, rushing down toward the earth, became visible against the brightening sky. It was a glider. At some two hundred yards it stopped its dive, slipped like a shadow over the trees and landed, plowing up the grass in the clearing with its landing gear. After a run of about fifty feet it stopped not far from Zvantsov.

Its belly opened up immediately, and ten dark figures spilled out. Zvantsov leaped up, raised his hand and, obedient to his command, they hastily and silently followed him into the woods. They came to the burned-out tank with its taunting, illiterate inscription made by a German hand and then proceeded with utmost care. There was a clearing ahead. Zvantsov divided his unit into three groups. Behind a tree stood the figure of a sentry in a black coat. Zvantsov drew a knife from its sheath, stepped toward the sentry lightly, as one does in a dream, pressed one hand over his mouth from behind and with the other plunged the knife into his neck. There was immediately a whistle behind him, and the men who had come with him made a dash toward the covered trucks standing in the clearing.

Soldiers in black coats ran out to meet them, and a short fierce battle ensued. One of the trucks suddenly flared with a scarlet light and exploded, scattering several figures in all directions. But Zvantsov with a revolver in hand was already fighting his way to another. A man was rushing back and forth near the truck, frantically striking a little box against it. Another, in the driver's seat, was trying to start the motor. Zvantsov fired at one, then at the other, and jumped into the seat of the truck. Without halting to push out the dead man, he pressed the starter, stepped on the gas, and just as a third truck exploded behind him, veered into a sharp, quick curve, and broke out of the clearing.

By now dawn was lighting up the sky. The forest road with shallow grass-grown ruts rushed to meet him. Swinging the truck from side to side, turning the steering wheel sharply, he sped to some destination that he knew. A group of men attempted to bar his way, but scattered, virtually from under the wheels, and the windows of the truck bloomed with rainbow-colored stars from a spray of bullets.

Then the forest rushed back, and a wide, open field flashed brightly before him. Ahead, somewhat below him, a battle was in progress. Tanks, tiny as toys in the distance, moved across the space; a battery was firing at them; soldiers ran from spot to spot in a brittle chain.

As though merged with the truck, Zvantsov plunged downhill along a road as serpentine as the mark of a whip, into the very center of the battle. The head of the dead man next to him kept banging against the cushion of the seat, but Zvantsov could not find a second to open the door and throw him out.

The battle drew near, and he could hear the clear rapid fire of machine guns. A line of trenches. Soldiers with astonished faces jumped up and raised their hands, trying to stop him. He flew past them, flew across a mine field, a mine blew up nearby, but he was already far away—he had broken through the line of the attackers. Again the rushing dirt road flung itself under his wheels in tense curves. It was not he who steered the truck, but the earth itself that was turning—flashing bits of horizon, shrubbery stretched in a long straight line, green wooded hillocks—turning frantically to steady his lightning flight.

At last another wood rushed in upon him with coolness and shadow. Branches swished over the roof of the truck. Zvantsov began to slow down, turned into a forest path, dashed up to a small hut and braked the truck.

Several men in civilian clothing ran out to meet him. The trees still rocked before his eyes; the clearing and the hut still seemed to flow. But he jumped out of the truck and with the civilians began to tear off its canvas cover. Under the cover was a large frame with lengthwise metal grooves.

Three other trucks drove in at high speed, and more people assembled around them, silently, without wasting a moment for words. Zvantsov and the civilians hurriedly tossed branches over the top of the truck he had brought and pushed it deeper into the woods, into the very thick, under the trees. Its canvas top was stretched over another truck. From somewhere, the men brought yet another cover and wooden frames. Three soldiers appeared, wearing green uniforms. They got into three new trucks and drove them out, one after the other, away from the hut, raising clouds of dust.

And all at once Zvantsov saw, not with his own eyes, but with another sight, a scene behind the front line he had just broken through. Small figures, wakened by alarm signals, ran across airfields toward planes; he heard the command, and the singing roar of starting motors.

A moment later, he was not only Zvantsov, but also the pilot of the plane. The earth dropped away, hung under him like a huge, concave bowl, and his eye was level with the horizon which had suddenly receded into a vast distance. And he, the flier, was closely peering below. Teeth biting into lip, he looked for something among the toy houses of the villages, the rounded carpets of wooded hills and copses, the narrow bright

40

paths. He caught a glimpse of a hurrying buglike vehicle with covered top on a forest road. This was what he needed. With sudden joy in his heart, he went into a dive, preparing to drop a heavy load of bombs.

Then Zvantsov was three fliers in turn, and destroyed, one after another, three trucks with covered tops which had been sent out from the clearing in the woods. But at the same time, he was also the earlier Zvantsov, the one who had remained with the first vehicle—the really important one, hidden deep in the woods, in which the driver he had shot was still lying across the seat. . . .

This dream came to Zvantsov three nights in succession and left him tormented and exhausted. He only needed to close his eyes to plunge immediately into the nocturnal fight with the men in black coats in the clearing; or else the road was rushing under the truck; or he was going up in the plane, pursuing the wrong truck.

On the fourth night came the crowning scene—the conclusion, as it were, of these dreams.

He lay down in the evening at headquarters, pulled off his boots, spread out his coat under him and slipped his head into his helmet. (Generally, he did not like the helmet and never wore it, but used it to sleep in, since its soft inner lining was almost as comfortable as a pillow.) He closed his eyes and instantly began to dream.

Zvantsov was in a train. The wheels clattered, the crossties ran and ran away from under them, and he knew that he was bringing and was about successfully to deliver something extremely valuable. The train stopped in an unfamiliar station. Two workmen in blue-gray clothes with the Nazi insignia on their sleeves were bending over the switch. Strange soldiers in fatigues stood at ease on the platform. The stationmaster, a white staff in his hand, ran forward to meet Zvantsov; he was

41

perspiring, and his face expressed fear and respect. Zvantsov waited for his explanations with cold and masterful contempt. . . .

Then the station vanished. He was in a large hall with a terrace on the right. There was no one in front of him. But behind him (Zvantsov knew) stood a silent, closely packed multitude of men, most of them in uniform: marshals, generals and colonels of the Nazi army. The room was quiet, but suddenly the quiet condensed into absolute stillness. The wide white door in front of him opened, and, with the sound of rapid steps, a man came in . . . Hitler! Hitler, with his moustache and forelock, dressed in a gray field jacket and breeches. Hitler came to meet Zvantsov, and the crowd of high officers stood with bated breath behind him. Zvantsov's whole body became taut as he prepared with a sharp mechanical movement to throw his arm forward in the fascist salute.

Hitler halted, his bony face pale. For a minute he looked at Zvantsov with frenzied, and at the same time tender, eyes. Then his eyes flashed a signal to someone behind Zvantsov. Two buglers stepped out, took up their positions beside Zvantsov on the right and on the left, inhaled deeply, raised their heads, and . . . a sharp cock's crow filled the hall.

The crowing woke Zvantsov.

It was the only surviving rooster in the village, which by some miracle had managed to live through the German advance of 1941 and the passing of SS units in 1942.

The rooster woke Zvantsov and he stared around him in bewilderment.

What could this mean? Why did he dream such things?

He knew that these dreams came to him by mistake, that they were alien dreams which could not rightly come to him, the Soviet soldier Zvantsov, but really belonged to someone else, and had somehow strayed into his head.

But whose dreams were they?

Sitting on the floor, he looked around him. Back from inspecting the defense, the gloomy Lieutenant Petrishchev, company commander, slept heavily. (He was almost always gloomy, for he had left his wife and two little daughters in Brest, and had not heard from them from the very outbreak of the war.) But Zvantsov knew Lieutenant Petrishchev well; he had served with him in Brest and was as sure of him as of himself.

Next to Zvantsov snored Vasya Abramov, Nikolay's partner in the reconnaissance. Abramov had come to the unit recently, after a stay at the hospital. From his stories, Zvantsov knew his entire biography, and he knew that this biography was true. Before the war Abramov had served in the Special Railroad Battalion of the Red Banner Baltic Fleet in Leningrad. It was an interesting military unit, perhaps the only one of its kind in the world. Near Leningrad there are two forts, Krasnaya Gorka and Seraya Loshad, linked with Bolshaya Izhira by a special railroad branch. The Special Railroad Battalion had been established to service this branch, along which arms and supplies were brought to the forts. It consisted of regular railway workers, but they wore navy uniforms and were considered a part of the Red Banner Baltic Fleet. While in this battalion, Abramov had often visited Leningrad on his days off and knew the city well. Zvantsov, himself a native of Leningrad, had had many occasions to verify his stories. (Abramov had even been to the new public baths on Tchaikovsky Street, which Zvantsov had helped build on the eve of the war as a foreman of a brigade of masons.) Besides, they were friends, they had been out together on many scouting missions, and each had often depended for his life upon the conscience and courage of the other.

There was another man sleeping at headquarters—the signalman Zorin. But he was a youngster, born in 1923, and all of him an open book; his cheeks were still covered with the fluffy down of youth, and he received frequent letters from his native village, with numerous regards from all his relatives.

None of these three could have been the proper recipient of the dreams which by some error had found their way into Zvantsov's head.

As he thought about this, Nikolay suddenly sensed that someone was staring at him from behind. He turned, and saw the Special Section man, Udubchenko, sitting by the wall, pressing his inevitable folder to his chest and looking at him with his pale eyes.

Then he rose, approached Zvantsov, and suddenly asked in a low voice:

"Do you know German?"

"No," said Zvantsov.

"And Polish?"

"No."

Indeed, Zvantsov knew no foreign languages. Once upon a time, he had had some German at school, but nothing remained in his head except *Ich habe, du hast* . . . and the German word for *stove—oft*; in fact, he was not even certain that this was the meaning of the word—it might have meant *often.*

Udubchenko looked at Zvantsov expectantly for a few moments, then said, "All right," and walked out of the house.

Zvantsov was suspicious. It might have been some sort of a password: "Do you know German?" "No." "And Polish?" But he realized that he could do nothing at the moment. Should he seize his automatic, aim it at the man, and shout that he was a spy? But why? How could he tell? "Because I am dreaming such strange dreams."

It made no sense.

Tortured by doubts, Zvantsov rolled a cigarette and struck a light. The top layer of the rough tobacco began to swell, crackle, and send off tiny sparks in all directions. He threw his army coat over his shoulders and went out.

A stupid, rotten dream! That he, Zvantsov, should stand at attention before that swine Hitler! Why, if he found himself anywhere near that beast, he'd tear him to pieces and trample the pieces into the mud. Into the mud, with his heavy boots. And then he'd go to the quartermaster and demand another pair of boots, and throw away the first pair himself.

Zvantsov inhaled deeply, shook his head to free himself of the dream, and looked around.

It was a fragrant, velvety, mild Ukrainian night. The smell of apple blossom and mock orange was in the air. But the village, bathed in bluish, phosphorescent moonlight was grotesque and ugly. The chimneys of burned-down houses raised their abandoned, useless columns in the graveyard silence, and everywhere—in the dark hulks of ruins, in the ravine behind the garden, in the distant copse behind the field—lurked danger.

The situation at the front was shaky, and Zvantsov knew that Nazi infantry might already be assembling beyond the woods, that an enemy scout might be looking at him at that very moment from behind last year's half-rotted haystack in the meadow.

But the main trouble was that there was no way of knowing where the enemy was, and where our own troops. No one knew which way the company must face to avoid a blow from the rear.

These thoughts sent a cold shiver up Zvantsov's back. He cautiously shielded his cigarette with his palm.

A shadow of a movement seemed to flicker at the far end of the garden among the apple trees. Zvantsov started and strained his eyes, peering at the spot. The movement was repeated. Trying not to step on twigs, bending low, he tiptoed forward and saw the deaf-mute girl, the old man's daughter.

Dressed in a gray homespun shift, barefoot, she was digging the earth with short and strong, but somehow abrupt and

45

clumsy thrusts. Next to her lay a large, crudely made box, and on it, a sack of grain.

Sensing Zvantsov's presence, the deaf-mute turned quickly and jumped aside, frightened.

Zvantsov looked at the pit, the box, and the sack. He understood that the old man and his daughter did not believe that the company would hold the village against the Nazis, and were burying the grain beforehand to keep it out of the hands of looters. He felt bitter and ashamed before the woman. He motioned her to give him the spade, spat at his palms and quickly dug a pit in the yielding garden soil. Together they lowered the box with the sack inside it, covered it with earth and trampled it down.

Zvantsov wanted to drink. He asked the girl for water, then realized that she could not hear him and tried to explain what he wanted in sign language.

She looked at him dully, without understanding. Then she beckoned to him, and they returned to the house. The deaf-mute bent down to the cellar window and made an inarticulate sound. A lantern wick lit up below, and the old man came up the stairs. As he was coming up, the moon shone on his bald head, fringed with long, unkempt hair.

When he heard that Zvantsov wanted a drink, the old man offered him tea and honey, and invited him down. Zvantsov refused at first, although the thought made his mouth water. He knew that this honey, the potatoes and the grain buried in the garden by the apple tree might be the only food the two would have for many months ahead.

While they talked, the intelligence man with his folder appeared behind the fence, and the old man said, looking at him with disapproval: "Hangs around here all the time. What does he want?"

Afterward the old man managed to persuade Zvantsov to come down for a cup of tea and led him into the cellar. The ladder, propped against the window from within, was narrow and shaky. The deaf-mute gave Zvantsov her hand to keep him from slipping in the dark. Her palm was meaty and unpleasant. At first she held it curved, like the peasants, but then Zvantsov felt her fingers take his hand with a strong and trusting grasp. This small caress warmed his heart; he remembered his wife and little son in Leningrad, from whom he had not heard for almost a year, and his eyes became moist in the darkness.

The cellar was large. One corner was piled from floor to ceiling with potatoes, which had begun to sprout pale shoots. There was a sour smell. At the other end stood two benches covered with rags, where the old man and his daughter slept. There were also a table and several large boxes. On the moist brick wall, a small discolored mirror in a wooden frame hung from a rusty nail.

The old man turned up the light by pulling up the wick and added fuel to the samovar, in which the water was already warm. They began to drink linden tea with honey. The conversation lagged; the old man was taciturn. Zvantsov learned that he had been a teacher, and noticed that his hands were, indeed, not a peasant's hands, but those of a city man engaged in professional work.

The deaf-mute stared at Zvantsov's face and smiled continually with a strange, mindless smile. The old man said that she had spent her whole life in a neighboring village, that she was illiterate and did not know sign language. Because of her disability and because he had just helped her to bury the grain, and both of them knew what this meant, Zvantsov felt constrained and somehow guilty before her and her father. He was anxious to get out of the cellar.

Above, over the wooden ceiling, they heard steps. The cellar was just beneath the room occupied by the company headquarters. Zvantsov said that the company commander had

47

come back and might need him. He thanked his hosts for the tea and climbed out into the street.

That same night artillery fire was heard in the rear of Zvantsov's battalion, and in the morning came orders from the division to hold the positions for three days, after which the battalion was to march east to join the division.

However, the Germans still failed to appear in the vicinity of the village. The gloomy Lieutenant Petrishchev's nerves were shot. He waited and was prepared for battle but the uncertainty was worse than any clear and definite danger.

In the morning Zvantsov and Abramov again went out to look for the enemy. They went to the copse where the German antitank battery had been positioned, then made a circle from south-west to south-east toward the wood which was to be held by a cavalry unit and which the scouts had never searched.

They found no military units either at the edge of the wood or for a mile within it. Zvantsov and Abramov followed the edge of the wood, so that the village where their company was stationed was left considerably behind.

The terrain was uneven. They climbed down into a ravine, littered here and there with blackened casings of fired shells, and then came up to where a line of old trenches ran along the ridge. Zvantsov suddenly had the feeling he had been here before and knew this place. He jumped across several half-collapsed communication passages interlaced with numerous gray telephone wires. Something black loomed between the trees. A strange premonition stung his heart.

In front of the scouts, leaning over a trench, stood the twin-turreted old tank of Zvantsov's dream. Along its bloated flank ran the inscription in crude, uneven letters, *The armar is strong, and our tanks are fasst.*

Zvantsov was so astounded that his whole back broke into a sweat, and he felt his blouse cling to his skin.

At once he saw the path into the wood, which he also remembered from his dreams.

He coughed and his throat suddenly went dry. He nodded to Abramov and they cautiously began to move along the path. They had not gone a mile when a sharp cry was heard ahead: "Halt! Hands up, don't move!" A man came out of the bushes with a Tommy gun aimed at them.

He wore a black military coat.

A marine coat.

"Who are you?"

"Our own," Zvantsov replied from behind a tree, where they had managed to jump back for cover. "Infantry reconnaissance. What unit is this?"

"Hands up!" another voice commanded.

The scouts looked back and saw another sailor behind them with an automatic.

"Clear out, fellows," said the first sailor. "This is a secret unit. It's out of bounds. Make it fast. Petrov, see them out."

The second sailor escorted them to the edge of the wood, and the scouts walked back to their company. But before leaving, Zvantsov caught sight of a large vehicle behind the trees, covered with branches.

It was already growing dark. Zvantsov walked sunk in the deepest thought. As they approached their village, Abramov began to recollect his own service in the navy and wonder what the secret unit might be. But Zvantsov was scarcely listening to him, thinking with horror that he no longer trusted either Abramov, or Petrishchev, or anyone he had spent the nights with at headquarters. Not even himself. The dream was passing into reality, and it seemed to Zvantsov that he was losing his mind.

Until late in the evening he grappled with the problem of whether he ought to tell the lieutenant about his dreams. Finally, coming to no decision and totally exhausted, he settled down on his usual spot on the floor. The room was noisy. Petrishchev doubled the guard; messengers arrived from the platoons, and the telephone operator maintained constant contact with the battalion.

Zvantsov fell asleep only in the late hours of the night. As soon as he closed his eyes, he was immediately looking into some blurred glass, a dusty mirror, which reflected a face. But again not his face, but someone else's. That face!

Something stung his consciousness. He woke and concentrated intensely for a moment. A thought flashed across his mind. He hastily arose, took his semiautomatic and went out.

The night was windy. The weather was turning nasty; the western edge of the sky was heavily overcast.

Zvantsov looked around, waited for his eyes to grow accustomed to the dark, checked his knife in its sheath, and briskly walked out of the village. He knew where the sentries were posted that night and, to avoid meeting them, he made his way across the gardens, now crawling, now making a fast run. Then the gardens were left behind. He came out onto a path that circled around the ravines. At first he stepped uncertainly, but when a field of sunflowers opened before him, Zvantsov knew he was going in the right direction.

He began to hurry. Frequently glancing back, he quickened his steps almost to a run. At the end of the field, he glimpsed a shadow flickering in front of him. Keeping it in sight, he followed it and drew up closer to it in the copse. It was the old man from the cellar. But now he had straightened up, and his gait was light and elastic. To make no noise, Zvantsov slipped off his boots. Suddenly he heard steps behind him. Hiding in the bushes, he saw the intelligence man Udubchenko slip past, pale, looking in all directions.

Zvantsov had expected his appearance. He let him pass and followed in his wake.

He crossed the wood, but in the wide clearing he saw only

the old man walking on the grass. Udubchenko had disappeared. Zvantsov doubled his caution, circled around the edge of the clearing and drew nearer to the old man when the latter halted, peering at the sky.

Zvantsov had already cautiously put his finger on the safety catch of his automatic to release it and glanced back, planning his action in the event of attack from the rear. Then something crackled under his foot.

The old man turned in his direction, but it was hard to tell whether he saw Nikolay.

A cloud had come over the moon, then freed it.

Zvantsov prepared to step behind a bush.

The old man, looking at Zvantsov, said something in another language, not Russian. And Nikolay received a crashing blow on the head. Something seemed to explode in his brain. He turned and saw, a step away, the old man's deaf-mute daughter with an elongated object in her hand.

His hands and feet went numb. He thought: this is how a man dies. But at that moment a deafening shot rang out. The bullet whizzed past Zvantsov and struck the old man, who grunted and doubled up. Behind the back of the deaf-mute woman appeared Udubchenko, who knocked her down with a single blow and rushed toward the old man.

Two minutes later everything was over. The old man and the woman, no longer deaf-mute, but viciously cursing in German, were lying on the grass, tied up with leather thongs. And Udubchenko, shivering with excitement and almost giggling, was saying to Zvantsov:

"The vermin! The vermin . . . You understand, I thought you were in with them. I'd nearly fired at you. I'd nearly killed you. . . ."

Nikolay, whose head was beginning to clear, picked up the flashlight dropped by the woman and crossed to the center of the clearing.

The German plane was already humming overhead, and Zvantsov was signaling to it when the black-coated sailors, roused by the shots, appeared in the clearing. They had been stationed in the neighboring wood with a battery of rocket-launchers or "Katyushas," as they came to be known later.

Zvantsov explained everything to them. After that, events unfolded exactly as in his dream.

The plane flew away. For a while everything was quiet. Then a light flashed in the sky. A huge black bird silently floated over the treetops. Creaking, the glider came down and ran along the clearing, tearing up the grass with its chassis wrapped in barbed wire.

The door opened.

But Zvantsov, Udubchenko, and the sailors were ready. A grenade was thrown and exploded. The Nazis, caught by surprise, did not even attempt to resist. Their entire unit was captured and, with the exception of those killed, delivered to Zvantsov's company headquarters.

In the morning the front came into action. Two German battalions supported by tanks struck at Petrishchev's carefully planned defense lines. Battered divisions of the Fifty-seventh Army and a division of rocket-launchers began to come out behind the village, escaping from encirclement. And the gloomy Petrishchev fought, covering their retreat. More than half of his company was destroyed, but it carried out its orders and left the village only on the third night, taking with it the wounded and the two still functioning cannons. Lieutenant Petrishchev also rolled a cannon, or, to be more exact, held on to its carriage. He was deafened, his head tightly bandaged. But he continued to give commands and instructions, which no one paid attention to. He was delirious.

Nikolay Zvantsov, however, took no part in the fighting and learned about the action later from comrades. With Udubchenko, the "old man," the former deaf-mute and the surviving German members of the landing unit, he was sent at once to the division headquarters, to the Special Section of the army. It turned out that the "old man" was a leading German spy and diversionist, and the false deaf-mute was his assistant. They had been left behind by retreating German units with a special assignment: they were to steal our new weapon—one of the "Katyushas," the power and importance of which Hitler's staff understood even then.

The Nazi spy had discovered the battery and had called out the German landing party over the radio hidden in the potato pile in his cellar. But before he had called, he had planned the operation carefully, going over all the details again and again. In fact, he had thought about it constantly, visualizing exactly how it would take place, how he would take the "Katyusha" across the front lines, and even how he would deliver it to Germany and receive his reward from Hitler's own hand. He imagined all these scenes at night, sitting in his cellar under the company headquarters, and the pictures he evoked had in some incomprehensible fashion communicated themselves to Zvantsov, appearing in his dreams. Indeed, Zvantsov had spoken in his sleep—in German and Polish—arousing Udubchenko's suspicions.

It is possible that the Nazi's hopes and ambitions were so intense and passionate that they somehow created a field of electromagnetic forces that we still know nothing about. But it is more likely that the reason for the strange dreams was not in the quality of the spy's emotions, but in some special abilities that had suddenly manifested themselves in Zvantsov. After all, many other people had slept at the company headquarters above the "old man," but the dreams came only to Nikolay. Besides, there had also been that earlier occasion with the "polygon."

At the army's intelligence section, Zvantsov also reported his first dreams, about the truck with the milk cans and the

53

truck driver. And the spy testified that these scenes belonged to his memories of the summer of 1939 in Poland, on the eve of the war, when the Germans had already begun to deliver arms and store them in German estates on Polish territory, preparing a Nazi fifth column. On the night when Zvantsov had dreamed about the park and the crypt where the arms had been hidden, and about the driver who was beaten, the "old man" had been thinking of the occasion when he had almost been betrayed by a Polish truck driver. (The little windowless lodge had indeed been a crypt.)

The intelligence officers were amazed at Zvantsov's ability to sense other people's thoughts and wanted to keep him at headquarters, so that he might dream the thoughts of the German prisoners of war who were loyal Nazis and refused to give information. But Nikolay no longer dreamed anything. He felt out of place at headquarters and asked to be sent back to his unit. In the end, his request was granted.

Udubchenko remained with the Special Section, where he turned over his Underwood and his file. He was assigned to service with a lieutenant colonel and eagerly took up his duties.

Such was the story that Nikolay Zvantsov told us during the long evenings in February of 1943 when we were in the convalescent battalion, on Zagorodny Prospect, opposite the Witebsk Station in Leningrad. . . .

3

The Golden Lotus, A Legend

By M. GRESHNOV

"So you don't believe it?"

"I certainly don't!"

"But what about Tibetan medicine? And legends? And songs?"

"Legends? They will remain legends. Like the legend of the golden cave that was found to contain no gold at all. As a geologist, you ought to know it. Forget your cave lotus. Enough of fantasies, my friend, enough of fantasies!"

This conversation took place at the Geological Institute of the Urals Branch of the Academy of Sciences between Pavel Ivanovich Alabiev and Dmitry Vasilievich Sergeyev, head of our expedition to Pamir.

Others present were the young geologist Anatoly Frolov, assistant to the head of the expedition, and myself. I sat across the table from Anatoly and saw a tempest of feelings reflected in his face. His eyes, full of eager interest in everything around him, took fire as soon as the cave lotus was mentioned. When Alabiev argued against it, Anatoly's eyes darkened. Once or twice he was on the verge of breaking into the discussion but restrained himself. When he heard the categorical ban on 'fantasies,' he slipped out of the room.

Sergeyev had learned about the golden lotus on his last visit to the capital. His old friend, Academician Brezhnev, who was a doctor of medicine, was studying folk medicine and in his research on eastern remedies had often come across the mention of cave lotus. Hearing that Sergeyev was going to Pamir, Brezhnev persuaded him to look for the lotus, which, according to his information, could be found in only three places on earth: Pamir, the Himalayas, and Tibet.

"Just think, Mitya, what a service it would be to science! This lotus has inexhaustible possibilities: it heals wounds, blindness, leprosy. And, Mitya, it is, after all, only a plant! We shall cultivate it, like ginseng—whole plantations of it!"

And the old scientist launched into an enthusiastic lecture on the future plantations of the marvelous flower.

Then suddenly—"Enough of fantasies, my friend!"

A week later our expedition was already in the mountains of Pamir.

In Khorog, the last city on our itinerary, we broke up into two unequal groups. The smaller group, led by Sergeyev himself, went north, along the right tributary of the Amu-Darya—the Bartang, which is known in its upper reaches as Murgab. This group was to prospect for asbestos deposits. My group, consisting mostly of younger men, went eastward, to the Zor-Kul Lake and the sources of Pamir-Darya. Under my leadership, the team was to study the lake region and obtain ore samples.

Anatoly, as a specialist on asbestos, should have gone with Sergeyev. But he flatly refused.

"Why?" asked Sergeyev. "Your training is needed in this group."

"I beg you, Dmitry Vasilievich, I beg you, send me to Zor-Kul."

"I see no reason to do so. You will come with us to Murgab."

"Dmitry Vasilievich! Comrades!" Anatoly appealed to everyone, turning pale with excitement. "Let me go to

Zor-Kul! I've been there before, I know every path. I am sure to find asbestos there as well! Let Raya Aksenova go with Dmitry Vasilievich—she knows as much as I do about asbestos."

He looked at Raya with anxiety and hope.

Everyone interpreted Anatoly's request in his own way; some thought it a whim, others felt it logical: he had been at Zor-Kul, he knew the region.

Raya was hesitant. But, seeing that everyone was waiting for her answer, she said at last:

"Very well, I'll go to Murgab."

Sergeyev had little choice but to consent and permit Anatoly to join the Zor-Kul expedition.

Several days later after supper at camp I briefly discussed the next day's tasks with my group and, wishing the young men and women good night, retired to my tent.

For some reason, no one else around the campfire stirred.

"Remember, we are starting at five tomorrow morning," I warned and lowered the flap of the tent.

As a rule, I fall asleep instantly. But that night sleep would not come. The conversation around the fire was concerned with the most ordinary things: rucksacks, boots, geological maps. The girls began to argue about hairdos. Someone quipped that a geologist's best hair style is a close clipping. The boys laughed, and one of the girls called the wag a camel.

"Shall we start?" a loud voice asked, and there was immediate silence. "Let us start, comrades!"

I recognized Anatoly's voice. There was tense silence around the fire. I listened carefully.

"I propose," said Anatoly, "that we dispense with minutes at this meeting: let each one make his decision and carry it out as his conscience dictates. And there is only one question I will put on the agenda: the question of the lotus."

"What?" I almost cried out and sat up. Anatoly meantime went on:

"Dmitry Vasilievich was ridiculed at the Institute and warned to do the job and to forget the fantasies about the lotus. But there is nothing ridiculous about it. I am firmly convinced that the lotus exists, or existed in these regions, and I have—" he paused as though to take a deep breath, "I have indications—"

"Explain!" somebody cried out.

"I will," said Anatoly. "In 1958 I worked with an expedition in this area, in the upper reaches of Amu-Darya, but higher up, on the plateaus leading to the Sarykolsk Range. We met many native shepherds and often sat by their fires and listened to their songs, riddles, and legends. That was when I first heard about the cave flower. I wondered at the great number of legends and tales about the flower. An old shepherd once asked me: 'Why do you keep looking for stones and iron? Iron may make a man's hands stronger, but it will not add to his days. Why doesn't anybody look for the wonderful flower that grows in caves and never sees the sun, but can fill an aged body with sunshine? This flower exists in our mountains. My grandfather knew the cave. He plucked the golden flowers and that was why he lived to see my own father's head turn gray. And my father was the youngest of his fourteen sons!' It is said that this lotus grows in the dark, in the water, that it drinks spring water and is therefore transparent like a mountain spring, and when it is brought into the light it bursts into flame and burns up, leaving behind only a wisp of golden smoke. . . ."

"It's a fantasy all right," laughed one of the girls. "Burns up, hah!"

"Wait!" cried the others. "Don't interrupt!"

"We questioned the old man," Anatoly went on, "where this cave was and how it could be found. It is somewhere in the east, under three jagged cliffs, and the entrance is under the middle one. Then, far from those regions, I heard from other people about the three cliffs and the cave under the middle one. And once, from a high plateau, I saw through my field glasses a mountaintop with three cliffs. I think it's in the mountain ranges on the Chinese border."

Everyone was silent, then all began to speak excitedly at once. But Anatoly had evidently raised his hand, and they were quiet again.

"Brezhnev is a great scientist. He works on the problems of folk medicine, he has been to China and Tibet. The people there say that the cave lotus definitely exists, and ancient medicine considered it one of the most potent remedies. Why should this be a fantasy? I think that Academician Brezhnev is right, and I propose that we search for this flower!" Anatoly concluded firmly.

"And where shall we get the time?"

"We must combine the search with our regular work."

"And what is the chief going to say?"

"Alexander Gurievich said nothing at the Institute—either for or against."

"We'll look for it ourselves!" several voices cried eagerly.

At this point Yulia Krutova spoke up:

"He'll let us do it," she said with conviction, "especially if we explain it to him properly. . . ."

I was amused: it is rarely that you hear your subordinates' true opinion of yourself. I laughed, "If we explain it to him properly . . ." Well! My fledglings! Let us see how you will do it!

"So it's decided," Anatoly summed up. "Does everyone agree to the search?"

"Everyone!"

"Yes, yes!"

"Who is in favor? Raise your hands! Unanimous. The meeting is closed."

The next morning, like every morning in camp, was full of

bustle and haste. Tents were rolled up, rucksacks filled, packs loaded onto the horses' backs. The men shouted directions. The cooks were busy over the fire. At breakfast there were a few moments of quiet. This was the time I chose to strike. When everyone was concentrating on drinking tea, I asked with the most innocent air I could muster:

"So you have decided to look for the cave lotus?"

All eyes turned to me in confusion, waiting for my next words.

"We thought you were asleep," Yulia Krutova said naively, but no one even smiled.

My hopes of confounding them fell flat. All that remained was to tell them my decision.

"I have no objections. But we must agree on one thing: the work comes first and must not suffer."

They answered with a loud "Hurrah!"

On the ninth day of a difficult and exhausting trek we emerged into a wide, flat valley, surrounded by high ranges that reared their peaks in strange disorder. In the center of the valley was a lake, bright blue and welcoming, and everyone's spirits rose. It was the Zor-Kul Lake, and the valley was called Boli Dunyo, which means "The Roof of the World." It was truly the world's roof—at an altitude of four thousand meters! It was here that we were to work until mid-August, when the first snowstorms hit the peaks.

It is said that every spot on earth has its own face.

The face of Pamir is harsh and awe-inspiring. Mountains and mountains, endless granite chains. Huge stony monsters, upturned by an immense explosion. Black abysses. And at the summits—snow and ice. Wherever you look, menacing peaks encased in glacier ice.

There is a special, primeval splendor in all this, but it does not gladden the eye. The mountains are oppressive in their power, emphasizing the puny insignificance of man before the grandeur of the peaks and the elemental forces of nature. The face of the earth is still shifting, still in the process of formation here; enormous landslides, avalanches, instant earthquakes change the landscape suddenly before your very eyes.

In summertime, the valleys—now broad, now narrowing to a mere path locked between the mountain walls—teem with life. Here and there, blue rivulets of smoke stream upward into the sky. At night, the shepherds' fires glow everywhere like fallen stars.

We made our camp on the shore of the lake, and on the following day began to explore the valley. The young people lost no time: they questioned the shepherds about the mysterious lotus, struck up friendships with the native youths. And very soon the rumor spread throughout the valley like a mountain echo, reaching farther and farther into other valleys and pastures: people had come in search of the cave flower, transparent as a mountain spring and bursting into golden flame when brought into the sunlight. Soon there was not a single shepherd camp or village where this event was not discussed, where people did not recall all that they had ever heard about the wonder flower.

One sultry afternoon a slender, dark young man rode up at a swift gallop to my tent. Reining in sharply at the entrance, so that his horse reared, the young man cried:

"I bring word!"

I rose to greet him:

"Speak."

"Who is looking for the golden flower?"

"We are!" the geologists surrounded him.

"I know who can tell you about it," the rider said, his black eyes flashing.

"Who?"

"My grandfather, Artaban Sagadayev."

"Where is he? Where is Artaban Sagadayev?"

"He is herding flocks not far from here."

Two of our boys rode off with the guest to invite the old man to the camp.

The head of the Sagadayev clan came with his youngest son and grandson. Outside the camp they stopped, and the younger men helped the old man to dismount. Artaban Sagadayev, still erect and tall, walked, leaning on his son's shoulder. His eyes, intelligent, keen, and sparkling with ready laughter, showed that, while the old body still had much life left in it, his true strength lay in his mind and great experience.

"Welcome," Yulia Krutova greeted him for the rest of us.

Dinner was followed by an unhurried conversation about life, Moscow, our work, Pamir. Anatoly came over several times and sat down next to me, peering attentively into the old man's face, as though trying to guess whether the shepherd would be able to give us an answer to the riddle. The old man smiled and asked, "Who is this young man with the restless soul that cannot be contained in the dark depths of his eyes?"

I told him.

And when our bowls were filled with fragrant tea and had been emptied once, and twice, the group fell into the pensive, listening mood so characteristic of nights around a fire. At such moments you wait for something extraordinary—in the whispering of the night itself, or in the words of men. You expect the words to be magical, profound, full of mystery and inner awe.

And when this moment came and looked into the soul of everyone around the fire, Yulia Krutova raised her large candid eyes and turned to the guest:

"Please tell us about the miraculous cave flower. Your legends speak about it. Is there really such a flower, and how can it be found?"

"Yes, yes, do tell us," everybody echoed. We listened silently as the old man began his tale:

It happened in the days when Iskander the Conqueror crushed the thousand-year-old power of the Iranian Darius dynasty and, hoping to vanquish the whole world, came to the banks of our own Amu-Darya, which was then known as the Oks. But he had come in a black hour! Everyone rose up to defend his land, his water, his belongings, and his family. Men stood at their thresholds with swords and spears. But Iskander's iron warriors were pitiless. They killed all, even the boys, to make sure of their rule for centuries to come. They spilled the blood of the people like water, and the waves of the Oks turned red as sunset.

In the valleys of Pyandge, along the middle course of the Amu-Darya, there lived and labored the small tribe of Tadhais. Its people irrigated the fields, cultivated grapes and fruit, and pastured its herds in the plains of the Five Rivers. It was a peaceful but proud tribe. It refused to be enslaved by the invaders. And everybody took up arms.

But the forces were unequal. Iskander's warriors drove them up the river and pursued them, forcing them farther and farther into the mountains, across this very valley of Boli Dunyo and the blue lake of Zor-Kul, and still higher, into the black ridges of Sarykol.

All the people of the Tadhai tribe—men, women, and children—climbed the steep cliffs in the hope of discovering at least a small green valley. Yet they found no valley. Menacing clouds coiled and thundered around them, lightning flashed constantly like the arrows of enemies. Then suddenly, in its bright glare, everyone saw the black maw of a cave, and over it, like a dragon's crest, three huge, jagged cliffs.

The cave was dark, and the people did not dare to step inside it. They dropped at its mouth and, huddling together for warmth, fell into the troubled, bitter sleep of exiles. For many days the Tadhais sat there, afraid to go deeper into the dark womb of the cave. Inside the cave, in the eternal twilight, a lake gleamed faintly. Neither wave nor ripple broke its calm, but a brook flowed out of it.

The Tadhai tribe began to starve. Bold men ventured out from time to time into the mist to look for food, but they either failed to return, slipping down to their deaths from icy slopes, or else they came back empty handed. Then the elders of the tribe—old men as ancient as the rocks—went into the cave and sat down in a circle to take counsel on the shore of the lake. And a dreadful thought was born among them. They said: "Let us sacrifice the young maidens of the tribe to the gods. Let us throw them into the lake."

The maidens rose, bowed to their dear ones, and slowly walked toward the lake.

"Wait!" a ringing voice cried out. "Why should we all die?"

The speaker was Alan-Gyul, the most beautiful girl of the tribe, the daughter of old Gular, a poor man to whom the sun had given little light even in the Pyandge Valley. He had owned neither land nor water, and had labored all his life for other men. Alan-Gyul stopped the girls and came forward, tall and slender, with burning eyes. The elders moved menacingly toward her, thinking that she meant to stir rebellion against the will of the gods. But she looked at them fearlessly and said:

"Let me die alone to save the others. People have loved my beauty. Perhaps it will please the gods as well."

She bowed and proudly went to the lake, dissolving in the darkness. When people heard the splash, their hearts were filled with awe.

In the morning, when the mists cleared away, when the blue sky looked into the cave and the dark receded into its depths, the friends of Alan-Gyul went to look at the lake. They saw large, pale-green leaves floating on the surface, and over each—a proud flower, large as the lotus, transparent as mountain crystal. Someone daring stretched out a hand and plucked a flower; it came easily, together with the stem and root, which resembled an earth nut. Someone's hungry teeth bit into the root, and found it edible. And everyone began to pluck the flowers and eat the roots.

Quickly the people gained strength and turned toward the exit from the cave. One of them took a flower with him and brought it outside, into the sunlight. And suddenly he cried out with astonishment and fear. The flower burst into flame and melted in his hands, turning into a golden cloud. In the cave, one of the sick men, wishing to cool his burning wound, laid the petals of the wonder flower upon it, and the wound healed instantly.

A new life began for the tribe. . . .

"And where is this cave?" asked one of the young men.

"There," old Artaban Sagadayev pointed eastward.

"Is there any other sign besides the three cliffs?" asked Yulia Krutova.

"There is," he answered. "It is said that a red light, a rosy mist sometimes sways and drifts over the cliffs. . . ."

"A red light! A rosy mist!" cried Anatoly. "But I have seen them, I have seen them!"

In the morning, after the guests had gone, the group decided, before scattering to the various work sites, to speed up the work in order to complete it ahead of schedule and gain five or six days for the search for the legendary flower.

The events that followed disrupted our plans.

One day Anatoly's group returned from the eastern rim of the valley with the usual results of a day's explorations. But Anatoly's conduct struck everyone: excited and overwrought, he avoided his comrades, answering their questions absently and beside the point. No one could understand what was happening to him.

Fedya Bychkov was working at the radio, as usual. Anatoly sat down near him. Fedya said: "Talk of the devil . . . There's something for you . . . Something about asbestos. . . ."

At this moment, there were cries from the lake:

"Hold it! Hold it! Let out a bit! Oh, the devil, more, more! Now pull, pull! O-ho!"

Someone had caught a fish and, judging from the exclamations, a large one. Fedya, a passionate fisherman, heard the cries despite his earphones.

"Take it, Anatoly!" he begged, giving him the pencil and the earphones, and jumping out of the tent at one bound.

Anatoly sat down at the radio.

There was a message from Bartang: one of the group members had fallen ill, and they needed another specialist on asbestos. Sergeyev was asking for Anatoly and wanted to know how soon he could come. Anatoly wrote down the message word for word, and gave an immediate answer: "I am leaving. Expect me in ten days."

Fedya helped the young men to pull out a huge fish and returned to the radio. Anatoly handed him the record of the conversation.

"Report it to Alexander Gurievich."

Fedya glanced at the request and Anatoly's reply and looked up with astonishment. He had never expected Anatoly to abandon the search. He asked indignantly:

"And what about the flower?"

"Let them look for it without me," Anatoly answered calmly.

Fedya flew into a rage and cried:

"So you're ducking out! A fine enthusiast. . . ."

Anatoly silently withstood the annihilating look of his friend, shrugged, and went out of the tent.

The news of Anatoly's sudden departure instantly spread throughout the camp. Everyone talked about it. Everyone condemned Anatoly. To leave when the realization of the dream appeared so near! Some secretly swore to him that they would intensify the search, but he was deaf to everything and hurriedly prepared for the journey. Then Yulia Krutova remarked pointedly:

"I know, it is Raya Aksenova's work. . . ." And she sang out to the tune of a merry Rumanian song, "Nothing can divide them!"

But Anatoly, who had formerly been so morbidly sensitive to any joke at his expense, maintained a calm reserve.

Yulia came over to him and asked earnestly:

"What do you have in mind, Anatoly? Tell me honestly."

He replied, scowling:

"I am carrying out orders."

Anatoly made his preparations, and there seemed to be no reason to detain him. The telegram lay on my desk, and our work was drawing to an end. Anatoly did not wait for the horses which were to arrive in three or four days for the samples we had collected, and set out on the following morning.

Yulia and I escorted him out of the camp.

He took with him a rucksack with provisions, a flask, and an ice-axe.

"What's the ice-axe for?" I asked.

"Oh, it may come in handy, Alexander Gurievich," Anatoly replied without raising his eyes.

We said good-bye. Yulia walked a little farther with him, then fell back and returned with frightened eyes.

"He's acting strangely. Really, like someone possessed. We shouldn't have let him go, Alexander Gurievich. We shouldn't!"

But it was too late.

Camp life went on as before. Groups returned, bringing samples. They replenished their provisions and went out again. The geological map was being covered with new markings.

The Pamir summer was at its height. Dozens of brooks and rivulets carried streams of muddy water to the lake from the melting snows above. The Pamir-Darya, which flowed out of Zor-Kul Lake, rushed noisily westward, and its noise in the evenings was like a cradle song to us in the camp, to the herdsmen in the steppe, and to the herds wandering on the plain.

One night we were awakened by subterranean shocks and crashing thunder in the mountains. The walls of the tents shook. Our dishes and instruments clattered. Everyone jumped up. The plain resounded with the panic bellowing of the cattle. And from the surrounding mountain ranges came an incessant, deafening roar.

There is nothing worse than an earthquake in the mountains, especially at night. It seems to you that the cliffs are cracking and splitting open, and moving in from all sides, directly at you, threatening to collapse and crush you with their weight. We stood near the tents, huddled together and unable to control the chattering of our teeth and the trembling of our limbs. And the mountains crashed and thundered without end. Luckily, no one was hurt: all the herdsmen were in the plain, and the geologists in the camp. Besides, the earthquake touched the Boli Dunyo valley only with its outermost edge; its epicenter was in the east, beyond the Sarykolsk range.

A few more days passed. Our group prepared for the return trek.

Then one day, just before noon, a strange herdsman galloped into the camp on a horse covered with lather. He jumped off almost before reining in and shouted:

"Who's the chief? Where is he?"

I came out.

"What is it?"

"Is this yours?" he asked, handing me a flask.

The flask was bent, its sides crushed, with traces of silt and clay in the dents.

"Where did you find it?" I asked.

"There," he nodded eastward. "In the Kiik-Su river."

We were surrounded by all the members of the group. Yulia Krutova snatched the flask from my hands:

"But, Alexander Gurievich—" her breath failed. "It is Anatoly's flask!"

"Impossible! Anatoly went west!"

"Alexander Gurievich! It's his, it is—" and Yulia broke into childlike, helpless sobs, and dropped onto the grass.

Everyone stood dumbfounded.

"We found it on the shore," said the herdsman. "There are papers in it."

"Papers?"

I took the flask, unscrewed the lid, and looked in. There were indeed papers there. We had to break it with an axe, and found a copybook, without covers, torn apart: it was evidently too large to have been wedged through the narrow mouth of the flask.

The pages were covered with writing in indelible pencil. Anatoly's confession.

"I know I was wrong. But from the moment I saw the three cliffs again I could no longer control myself—

"In the beginning of July we came to an area explored by the expedition of 1958. I began to look for the mountain from which I had caught my first glimpse of the cliffs, and I found it. Then I came here again in secret, before sunset, and began to study the distant range through my field glasses. And finally I saw the cliffs. Old Artaban is right: immediately beyond the crest there rises a red mountain wall, and when the rays of the setting sun strike it, it seems covered with blood. And at twilight puffs of mist rise from the clefts, and that is the rosy smoke he spoke of.

"I returned to the group, but said nothing about it. I decided to discover the golden cave lotus alone, by myself. And when I received the call from Murgab, I went out toward the three cliffs.

"I found the cave. It is large, but not large enough to shelter hundreds of people, as the legend says. There is a stream in it. And a lake.

"I walked about twenty paces along the shore and noticed a wide circle on the surface of the water. I dropped to my knees and peered at it, and then I saw it was a large pale leaf, and over it rose a transparent, a totally transparent flower.

"I took its stem and pulled it. It came up easily, together with the root. I stood up and carried the flower to the exit from the cave. It seemed to come alive. First there was a faint flickering, then the outlines of the petals defined themselves. A lotus. Unquestionably, a lotus! Then the rims of the petals caught and refracted the blue of the sky: the flower glittered like silver and crystal.

"When I came out of the cave, the flower flamed in my hand! The sunlight, touching it, was caught and shivered in every petal, every curve. It filled the flower with hot fire and the flower began to melt. A fine golden mist rose over it. It seems that the flower consists purely of ether, and the warmth of the sun makes it evaporate. And the vapor is so dense and saturated that it reflects the sun and looks like transparent golden smoke.

"All that was left of it was the skeleton of the flower in my palm, made up of the finest gray gossamer threads. When I blew at it, it scattered into dust and dissolved in the air.

"For a long time I stood there motionless, stunned. My feet were bruised and broken, my shoes torn, and I was so exhausted I could scarcely move. After resting a while, I returned to the cave, plucked—or, rather, took out of the water—another flower and applied several petals to a bruise on my foot. They cooled it pleasantly, soothing the pain. Of course, the wound did not close up instantly, as the legend said, but the plant assuaged the pain. I cut off the root—a small bulb—with my knife and ate it. It has a pleasing taste, reminiscent of mint.

"I decided to describe everything I had felt and seen without delay. On the right, a narrow gorge led to the cave. The cave itself is small; its bed is covered with stones; it is about thirty meters deep, then it turns to the right. From this dead end, closed up with a pile of huge rocks, flows out the brook that falls into the lake and then continues out of the cave and down into the valley.

"I went to sleep in the cave, but was awakened by a frightful crash. The floor and the walls of the cave were shaking, and the noise grew and grew. I realized this was an earthquake and tried to rush out. But a landslide had closed the mouth of the cave. I was showered with stone dust and rubble. The lake splashed. And outside, it droned and droned, as though thousands of trains were rushing overhead.

"When everything was quiet again, I ran to look for my rucksack. I found my flashlight and turned it on. There was no exit. I cannot dig out of thousands of tons of rock by myself. The ceiling of the cave sagged and was cracked in many places.

"I sat down, put my head on my knees, and tried to think of nothing, to expect nothing. Then suddenly I heard the trickling of the brook. I traced its course: it flowed out under the rocks piled in the entrance. I noticed a faint glow of light over the water. I stared at it—it did not disappear. I thought I must be seeing things and closed my eyes. The light was gone. I opened my eyes—it was there again.

"A channel remained for the brook to flow through. I inhaled deeply and lay down in the water to examine the cleft. And far, far away I caught the dim glimmering of daylight. I pushed the ice-axe under the boulder, trying to widen the crack, but in vain. The rock is very hard, you cannot even chip away a splinter. . . .

"Before I perish here, I have decided to send out these notes. I will put the book inside my flask and drop it in the stream under the rocks. My flashlight is dimming, and I have no spare battery.

"Perhaps people will learn of my crime. Yes, yes! It was worse than a mistake. I deceived the group and withdrew from my friends. I went alone, spurning my comrades, and I perish ingloriously. A man alone cannot attain his dream. I shall now sketch the road that leads here and the plan of the cave. I shall put a lotus flower between the pages. This is all. Good-bye, my comrades! Good-bye, my friends! Good-bye, Alexander Gurievich! Good-bye, my dearest Raya!

"The lotus flowers are swaying before my eyes, glimmering mysteriously. But they exist, they exist! Don't lose hope, my friends, you shall find them! I put a flower between the pages.

"Farewell, my dear, beloved friends. . . ."

Anatoly's manuscript broke off. Between the pages I found the finest tracery of ash-gray veins—all that was left of the wonder flower. A handful of ash.

"We must search for him!" I ordered.

"Start at once!" Sergeyev confirmed the order over the radio.

But Anatoly's hastily sketched route on the last page of the notes was pressed against the wall of the flask, and the water that had seeped in washed away the violet lines of the indelible pencil, turning the drawing into a formless stain. We could barely guess at the spurs of the Sarykolsk range, and only at the lower right was there a clear outline of the elevation from which Anatoly had seen the three cliffs. The young men who had worked with him recognized the spot, and we decided to begin the search from there.

The next morning all the strongest men went out across the plateau to the spot marked by Anatoly. Three days later they returned. Their field glasses had failed to find either the cliffs or the red slopes. The earthquake, centered in Sarykol, had evidently altered the terrain.

Then we rushed out to explore the Kiik-Su river and all its tributaries. Several dozen streams flowed into it on both sides; there were also brooks which carried water only after rains. We followed every one of them. Many times we halted before red cliffs, but found neither the brook, nor the cave. We went on and on, encountering streams flowing out from under rocks. We reached the very source of the Kiik-Su, but all in vain.

Of all the theories that were suggested, one was the most likely: the stream that had brought the flask to the Kiik-Su must have been one of the subterranean brooks that we had encountered. But which one?

We kept up the search for twelve days, but found nothing.

A helicopter was sent in, but even that did not help.

We had done everything we could.

And now I am waiting impatiently for the next expedition to Pamir.

4

My Colleague

By V. GRIGORIEV

The alarm clock rings. I open my eyes, hoping desperately that the clock will be an hour fast. But no, my second clock is also pointing to seven.

I bought the second clock when I became absolutely convinced that one was not enough to wake me. Sometimes I thought that even three clocks would not do it.

On waking up, I still feel quite fresh. But after several minutes of struggle with sleep, I get up exhausted, with no desire except to be back in bed. What can I do? My scientific work leaves me less and less time for rest. I even dream about it. Even janitors in my dreams mumble formulas as they sweep the pavements.

If one is not to fall behind those who set the pace in science, one must work as much as they do. So it is really the great men who are to blame. And they sleep—heaven knows how little they sleep!

I remember—it was the need for a third alarm clock that forced me to give all this some really serious attention.

Now look, I said to myself. You are an adult, the author of many discoveries, an inventor. Can't you do anything about this humiliating, degrading, downright amoral condition we call sleep? When a man is asleep, he can be run over by a car, beaten up by a gang of rowdies, thrown out of a tenth-floor window, spat on. And he? He wakes up, washes his face, and

74

goes on as if nothing happened. Indeed, to whom can he complain?

These thoughts came to me more and more frequently, but I turned to the problem in earnest only after I had awakened several times fully dressed. That was too much. And then I made up my mind.

Naturally, no one can achieve total liberation from sleep entirely by himself.

Electrosleep, gravitation-sleep, radio-sleep, flatfoot-sleep —some day all these experiments will unquestionably lead to success. The many scientists in large modern laboratories who have been assigned to work on this problem are certain that the solution is no more than two or three decades away.

Of course, in relation to eternity such figures are but an instant. But to me this instant meant the best part of my creative life. And since science had not yet provided me with an absolute substitute for sleep, I gave some thought to devising a partial substitute.

An equivalent, a biological equivalent—this was what I had to seek. Let someone else sleep for me. Let the processes within the sleeping brain take their usual course, let their results be fed into a special receiver, and relayed through a transformer in purified form to my waking and thinking brain.

Of course, it was no easy task to find a man who would agree to sleep both for himself and for me. My circle of acquaintances was limited to men of science, charming absent-minded people whose mildness turned to granite whenever circumstances suggested an extra hour of sleep. The man I needed was different, a man of another sphere, so to speak. In short, a man who did not care how long he slept.

I found him in the street. Or, to be more precise, in a tavern. He sat at a table alone, and a glass with some liquid—most likely, alcoholic—trembled in his right hand.

"Science has broken all its teeth on me," he said when I sat

75

down at his table. "It treated me and treated me, and nothing ever came of it."

He was silent for a while, shook his head, smiled, exhibiting a gold tooth, and added:

"It tried to cure me of alcoholism. . . ."

"My friend," I began with utmost gentleness. "If science could not help you, perhaps you could help science?"

"It did not help me, and I will not help it," my new acquaintance mumbled drunkenly.

"But what if you tried just once more?"

"No, my friend, whoever you are, you won't tempt me with your sugared pills. One eats them and eats them, and then goes wrong all over again."

I spent a long time explaining my plan to this man, still young, but retired because of chronic alcoholism. And the morning (is there anything a truly logical approach will not accomplish?) found him sleeping in my apartment.

When he awakened, his first request was for some salt water. Then he looked around the room, lit a cigarette, and did not seem in the least surprised at waking in an unfamiliar place. He was evidently accustomed to waking up anywhere but in his own home.

"Does your head ache?" I asked.

"It does. If I could only fall asleep, but I won't—I know from experience."

"That's very easy to arrange," I answered at once, and pointed to the apparatus which stood innocently in the corner.

Naturally, my future teammate had completely forgotten the conversation of the previous night, so I warmly repeated all my arguments. I spoke of the need to speed up the progress of scientific thought. I brought in all the working models of my latest inventions—flying, crawling, diving, running, calculating, and computing—and also the model of an invention I was still working on—which would fly, crawl, dive, jump, and compute all at the same time. I emphasized the benefits to be derived from the use of all these devices and promised that one sample of this new machine would be given to him as virtual co-author and collaborator.

The graphs, formulas and blueprints made little impression on the man from the tavern. But when my machines ran into the room and began to dance, fly, somersault, squeal, climb on our knees, and mutter all sorts of proposals, he began to soften up.

"All this is your work?" he asked with amazement, carefully removing from his neck a synthetic imp who had already managed to comb his hair and spray it with cologne.

"Colleague," I said to him—yes, this was the word I used for it was clear that the battle was won—"Colleague, just wait and see what happens when we go to work together. The intensity curve of—"

"I agree," he broke in, and asked me to switch on the sleep apparatus.

Need I tell you of the giant leap forward in all my endeavors? Others came home a little tired and took up their newspaper, waiting for supper. But I continued to work. Others went to movies, stadiums, cafes to relax their brains, but I needed none of it. My brain was as fresh as a newborn child's, and I worked again. At midnight, others tossed and turned, counting to a thousand to get their minds off the day's preoccupations. But I continued to manipulate figures and graphs, working the levers of the calculator, slipping the slide rule in and out, and hugely enjoying myself!

And to think that there was a time, I would say to myself triumphantly, when you cursed your insatiable thirst for work. Your head was splitting, your heart traced regular figure eights on cardiograms, your hair dropped out as though your scalp were an old shoe brush. And at those moments, all your hope was that the doctors would do something for you. Who else could help? But they had only one tune: air, fruit, light wine, and less and less work.

Less work indeed! And I would burst into loud, happy laughter, without fear of waking my teammate. He slept with the sleep of the dead.

The efficiency of the apparatus did not exceed fifty-one per cent, and therefore he had to sleep for me sixteen hours instead of eight. Add to that the eight hours of sleep he needed himself, and you have twenty-four hours!

Sometimes I woke him—on days when a significant new achievement was added to the record. He listened to my explanations and occasionally evinced some interest, trying to grasp details. He appeared to become increasingly aware of being a collaborator in an important and useful activity.

When I awakened him for the first time, he merely shrugged and grunted, "Oh, well, carry on, what's the difference?" A month later he was already taking pleasure in poring over the sketches and blueprints, tightening the nuts on semiassembled models, and watching over my shoulder as I filled page after page with formulas and equations. His eyes were becoming ever brighter and more intelligent—at times they even showed intense concentration, with a shade of that hard wisdom typical of analytic minds at the moment when a broad new formulation suddenly takes shape.

This is what uninterrupted sleep can do, I gloated to myself, but to him I would say:

"Colleague! I am certain that I shall be able to prepare you in time for admission to a technical college. No, why stop at that? I shall get you through some university programs, too!"

The latter was added from sheer enthusiasm, but the first part of the promise I firmly believed in. My logical approach and native powers of observation never deceived me. Two months went by in a state akin to intoxication, to weightlessness. When I delivered my weekly reports of progress at the institute, everybody simply shrugged.

"When does he manage to do all that?" I heard from the conference hall.

"In one week he cooks up enough computations and blueprints for a new dissertation," people said in the smoking rooms. "He's headed straight for the Academy."

"You are unrecognizable," the director said to me with a sly smile. "You even find time for an occasional movie, for excursions with the children, even for skiing. As for achievements! What has happened to you?"

"Well," I answered with an equally sly grin, "I guess it is the skiing trips. The fresh air does wonders for you. Listen to the doctors, my dear director!"

I felt that it was too early to announce my method. A few more months of experimentation upon myself, and then, when everything was entirely clear. . . . Of course, there were moments of doubt: perhaps I ought to tell? No, not yet. But the success of the method was obvious enough!

Then suddenly I found that it was not so obvious after all. One fine day not a single line was added to my equations. And not a single new bolt was added to the models. I simply did not feel like working. The same thing happened the next day. And the next. This was a surprise. I checked the apparatus. It was working as faultlessly as ever. Was I ill? The thermometer showed a normal temperature.

I forced myself to sit at my desk—to no avail. My eyes refused to focus, the lines seemed strange, as though they had been written by someone else. Still worse, I suddenly realized with horror that I was barely able to understand the equations which I myself had formulated only a few days earlier.

Driven by some unknown power, I rose from the desk and went out into the street. Passers-by flickered like figures in a speeded-up film; store windows and advertisements floated by. Suddenly I found myself at a table in a large room. A waiter was filling glass after glass, and I drank them down. I do not know how my feet carried me home. But what I saw in my study instantly cleared my head. My teammate sat at the desk, writing away in my notebooks!

"What are you writing there?" My tone was not too civil.

"Colleague," I heard. "There are errors in the manuscript. At first everything was correct, but in the last few days the computations went astray."

"Allow me!" I exclaimed.

"Everything is corrected, colleague," my teammate continued, smiling faintly and giving me no opportunity to recover. "You can see for yourself."

For a brief moment my usual clarity of mind returned and I understood: he was right. Indeed, the errors had already been corrected.

I sat in my armchair, and he sat in the other, while words—his words—came to me as from a fog. . . .

"You were not mistaken that time when you called me colleague. As you see, I understand all these schemes, blueprints, layouts and machines as well as you do. Evidently, the apparatus you invented transmitted to me the qualities and the knowledge stored in your brain. At the same time, it transmitted some of my characteristics to you—alas, not the best of them. Whether we like it or not, it happened. However, the work remains to be done, and it must not suffer. There is only one solution: now you will have to sleep, and I will work until we return to our original condition."

Good heavens, he even formulated his ideas in my own way! He spoke with my own intonations! I could argue with anyone else, but with my own logic?

"Yes, of course, the work must not suffer," I replied indifferently, and the apparatus was switched on again.

Now we alternated, replacing one another as though on

schedule. The work really hummed. What I failed to think through, my teammate did; if he made an error, I caught it. At particularly difficult spots, the apparatus was switched off, and we solved the problem together.

One thing did not let me rest: the knowledge that fifty per cent of the pleasure of work passed me by. Of course, I could without a second thought eliminate the apparatus. But who could tell with certainty when the subconscious would be entirely free of the unfortunate acquired characteristics? No, I wanted no more surprises. And so, during one of my watches, I realigned the mechanism of the apparatus in such a way that the sum of our processes would finally bring us back to our original and stable states. The reassembly proved complex and difficult, and took almost the entire waking time assigned to me. But then I fell asleep pleased and reassured.

Alas, my teammate was not a man to be deceived so easily. He noticed everything and spent all his waking time, in turn, to restore the apparatus.

And now came the battle of giants! He altered the apparatus to his advantage, and I—to mine. And all this was done silently, secretly, as though nothing were amiss. But we stopped greeting one another or exchanging opinions. Moreover, there seemed to be no end in sight; it was a struggle of equals!

The basic tasks were, naturally, forgotten. Both of us were entirely possessed by the need to win. Who was going to get the final word?

I was the first to yield. Whether I yielded, or merely saw the light I cannot say. I reassembled the screws and springs of the partly dismantled apparatus and woke my colleague. He was annoyed and angry.

"I believe I did not sleep my full time," he said coldly, turning over on the other side. "Do your job, go on. And I'll do mine."

I was silent a while, collecting my thoughts. Then I began

as persuasively as I could, trying to make every word count.

"Neither I, nor you can be satisfied with the existing situation. As a man of science, you must understand this."

"Yes, yes, a man of science!" he burst out. "And I do not want to be anything else. Don't try to convince me. . . ."

"I am not trying anything of the kind!" I flared up. "I am not trying to convince you to give it up. I am proud! I am proud that I created you. After all, we have demonstrated that anyone, even an ordinary fool, can change, if only he wants to. Every man's brain is open—open to growth, to enlightenment."

The sincerity of my words seemed to affect my teammate. He stood near the apparatus, alert, attentive as I spoke and spoke.

"So you believe that in principle it is possible for us to separate and live our own lives as scientists?" he asked.

"Unquestionably," I answered firmly. "We must sit down at once and work out the problem, at least in general terms."

Enough time has elapsed since that moment to allow me to weigh and evaluate everything before reporting publicly on the experiment that some may call fantastic. My first teammate is still active and energetic; men of science eagerly study his latest work; journalists often interview him. Neither he, nor I have any fear of the future. The apparatus which we built transmitted to him enough intellectual energy to last two lifetimes. At the same time, I was entirely relieved of the acquired hindrances to work.

The errors of the past were taken into account, and all my subsequent teammates passed through the apparatus without undue disturbances or psychological problems. When they separated from me, they were full of creative ideas and bold concepts. Some went into technology, others devoted themselves to theoretical disciplines. There was even a violinist who managed to worm himself into the program. Scholars, doctors of science, they are men of wide information and achievements. When we happen to meet in the street, we greet each other and stand for a long time, discussing the latest developments in the various sciences. At times we simply get together—a closely knit family. And during these evenings the air fairly crackles with brilliant talk! They are also fond of hearing again and again the story of my first experiment. When they want me to tell it, I pull out my old alarm clock and say:

"This is the source of it all. It just couldn't wake me. . . ."

5

Vanya

By V. GRIGORIEV

What a boy he was! You said to him "two times two," and he said "four."

"Twelve by twelve," persisted the doubters.

"One hundred and forty-four," came the reply.

"Define an integral," the most carping skeptics went on.

"An integral is . . ." and a clear definition followed.

And all that at the age of four. A tot, a baby, his abilities astonished famous professors and doctors of science. Even an academician took several hours out of his busy schedule to have a look at the boy. The academician also asked questions, gasped and marveled, and shrugged in disbelief. Then he pondered the phenomenon for a long while, and finally pronounced:

"Nature is infinite and full of paradoxes."

After which he gazed with concentrated attention at the wall and sank into profound silence.

"Ah, Professor," Vanya (that was the boy's name) said wearily, "what nonsense! Nature is harmonious; it is we who bring the paradoxes into it."

That was too much. The academician jumped up and, staring at the boy with something close to superstitious awe, began to back toward the door.

"Two times two is four! Tell everybody!" the boy cried gaily in parting.

That was Vanya. An extraordinary child. And what made it all the more amazing was that he had entirely unsuitable parents. Individually, each may have loved the boy, but somehow it never worked together. The father felt that the boy's genius came from his side of the family. The mother insisted on the opposite. The son smiled at them indulgently, but this did not make things any easier. The parents quarreled more and more frequently, and, whenever this happened, Vanya was banished to the basement.

The door was closed to the professors and academicians. And, quite naturally, the great wide public soon forgot Vanya's existence.

But the boy outwitted everybody. He installed electricity in the basement and spent his time playing enthusiastically with a child's constructor set. Yes, yes, an ordinary constructor set. But only until the moment when he put his hands on his first radio tubes.

He literally trembled when he first saw them; he realized immediately all the possibilities hidden in those toys. Of course, toys. After all, Vanya was only in his fifth year, and he did not know that radio receivers, television sets, motorcycles, cranes, trucks, and excavators were serious things. He thought that grown-ups were simply playing with them.

Vanya's father, a mechanic who worked in a radio and phonograph repair shop, brought his son broken tubes, triodes, condensers, and the boy took them apart, seeking out the hidden damages. The semiconductors were put aside in a special case.

One day, when the father looked into the basement, his son offered him a small box.

"Here," the boy said, rubbing his hands with satisfaction. "And this is only the beginning."

A small television set gleamed with its bluish screen in the father's hands.

"Well!" was all the father could say, shaking his head with admiration. Then he thought a while, and added, "I see the boy takes after me."

In the morning he showed the toy to his colleagues, winked slyly, and said:

"My work."

The true meaning of his words escaped the listeners, and the mechanic was promoted to a better job. Now his supervisors often took him aside, saying confidentially:

"Kuzma Serafimych, something isn't quite right here. We ought to devise . . ."

"Let me have it," Kuzma Serafimych would interrupt with cool assurance, taking the blueprints. Clearly, he was not a man to waste time in idle talk.

At home, the blueprints were silently handed to Vanya.

"A special assignment," the father explained, grinning.

Vanya would silently examine the diagram, then take a red pencil.

"Here, here and here—" the pencil danced over the sheets. "These must be changed!"

The boy worked with a will, demanding in return only functioning parts and books on the latest developments in technology.

But one morning the father came to the workshop and called his foreman aside.

"That's all," he said simply.

"All what?" the man was puzzled.

"That's all, I'm through with inventing," Kuzma Serafimych said with emphasis, and added mysteriously, "For family reasons."

"But w-why?" the foreman protested.

"Not for the next four years. Perhaps after that!"

The conversation was finished.

Of course, the foreman did not know that the day before Vanya had refused to take any more work.

"Papa," he said gently. "I cannot waste my time on trifles now. I've hit upon a real idea. Give me four years, and I will make a toy the world will gasp at. Four years!"

The father knew his son's iron character and did not argue. He merely asked with a conspiratorial air:

"Four? But perhaps we can do it in three?"

"No, I still do not command time," Vanya answered thoughtfully. Then he gave his father a quick look and asked: "What's your idea—what is time?"

"Time?" the father's forehead puckered in thought. "Well, it's when . . ."

"Again those inexact formulations!" the son broke in impatiently.

Kuzma Serafimych turned and carefully tiptoed out of the cellar. What he heard as he was closing the door was altogether incomprehensible:

"A minute lives sixty seconds. Yes, yes, lives—it lives—"

From this conversation, the specialist will gather at once that the extraordinary boy had decided to solve the riddle of time. But a man unaware of the subtleties of the connection between radio technology and theoretical physics would, of course, fail to see quite so plainly that Vanya had resolved to invent a time machine. Nevertheless, it was so.

Yes, Vanya had decided to construct a time machine. And he achieved his goal.

This may be difficult to believe, since there is no proof of it except my word. For I am the only witness to the facts of the case. I repeat, Vanya admitted no one to his dangerous experiments with the machine. No one but me, his childhood friend and next-door neighbor.

"People will learn about this, they will," he repeated every

time we concluded an experiment and ran out into the street
to play with the other children at their simple, time-worn
games.

Cossacks and robbers, the little magic stick—these games
relaxed us, made us, in a way, more like the rest of the children. But, of course, compared with the game invented by
Vanya, they seemed primitive and silly.

The machine allowed us to soar off to the enchanting vistas
of future ages, or to submerge ourselves in the depths of the
past. We particularly enjoyed the medieval tournaments. Mud
flew in lumps from under the horses' hooves, and the knights
in beautiful armor pummeled each other with swords and
broke their spears in jousting. Usually, everybody came out
alive. We would find ourselves a comfortable spot somewhere
nearby and turn the pages of the Walter Scott novel we had
brought along, comparing the descriptions with reality.

Naturally, after such adventures, hide-and-seek games in
the yard seemed like the cave drawings of savages next to a
movie screen. Incidentally, we had also seen these cave drawings being scratched on cave walls. That was during our visit
to hoary antiquity: those shaggy peasants hacked away at the
walls of the caves with such gusto that sparks flew in all directions.

Nevertheless, we played with the children in our yard as
well.

"It is necessary," Vanya would say. "Caution and caution
again. We must not seem different from the others."

He did not want the machine, still imperfect, to fall into
anyone's hands. "They will break it," he warned me, and I had
to agree with him.

When we reached the stage of delving into the past and
flying into the future, we decided to hold our sessions at night.
Neighbors who happened to be caught in the machine's sphere
of action would be carried along. When in the mornings the

time lever was returned to its normal position the neighbors would get up as if nothing had happened and go to work at their usual jobs. Each of them assumed that he had dreamed a marvelous, magnificent dream the night before. Those dreams contained much that was strange, of course, but dreams happen to everyone. . . . The neighbors were prudent and cautious people. And just to be on the safe side, they told nobody about their peculiar dreams. The secret remained secure.

One day, though, some devil seemed to nudge me in the ribs. At the streetcar stop I waited for one of our neighbors —the lanky, phlegmatic warehouse manager Klotikov— winked at him with a conspiratorial air, and said, as I followed behind him:

"He was all right, that fellow with the ostrich feather on his helmet and the alligator on his shield, wasn't he?"

The warehouse manager's whole body jerked as from an electric shock, and he stared at me with horror. Then he hopped into a passing streetcar and was carried off.

Vanya listened to the story with a glum face.

"Either we stop the experiments, or this will never happen again," he rapped out.

I understood my friend. Things were not easy for him. The machine was acting up. The last time out it had nearly fallen apart from overloading. We had just barely managed to get out of the Middle Ages.

At the same time, the situation at home was getting worse. His parents quarreled more and more frequently. Much more than in the days of the professors. And although a good deal of time had passed, they had not come to any agreement. That's how they were, Vanya's parents. If it were not for this. . . .

Everything happened suddenly. I came to Vanya's and we began to do our lessons. But we could not work. His parents were quarreling. It was impossible to calm them down. I

89

noticed that the wall mirror was already broken, and the tablecloth was pulled to the side. I also noticed that my friend's hands were trembling. Vanya hated these quarrels.

"Let him tell us!" Kuzma Serafimych suddenly shouted, catching sight of his son.

I picked up my cap and ran out. What happened after that can only be guessed at.

The disordered machine had been set for short-range action. Vanya ran up to it and pulled the lever to move time back at least two or three hours. He had already done this several times before to restore calm in the house. But his hands trembled more than usual. He tore at the lever, and time began to slip. Yes, it slipped back beyond the limits of Vanya's age. The machine disappeared, and so did Vanya. As for the parents, they merely grew younger by some twelve or thirteen years. And were, of course, carried off in different directions.

When I came to see Vanya on the following morning, it was all over. A quick glance at the rooms told me everything. Vanya had not been able to return from the past: the time restorer was off the machine at the moment of the catastrophe; it had been removed for repairs and was lying in the corner of the cellar. But I did not lose hope. After all, according to the iron laws of probability everything had to repeat itself. By force of these laws, the parents, grown younger, would have to meet and fall in love again. And the reborn Vanya would, of course, again construct the magnificent apparatus which humanity needs so badly—the time machine.

And, indeed, they met. I waited for them near the same clock tower where they had first met thirteen years before. I was jubilant. Everything was going splendidly. I hailed the perfect beauty of mathematical laws and the iron logic of events. Vanya would be born again! The machine would be recreated!

But what was this? The young man, so remarkably like Vanya's father, and the young woman, a copy of Vanya's mother, stood silently, looking at one another with distrust. And suddenly they turned and walked away in opposite directions. Beads of sweat stood out on my forehead. Apparently, the memory of each retained the future that lay in wait for them.

And so, alas, the boy was never born! Lost for eternity. And with him, the precious time machine!

6

Last Door to Aiya

By E. PARNOV and M. YEMTSEV

At night there was a sudden downpour, which went on and
on. Lightning tore dazzling gashes in the black sky, and it
seemed to Yegorov that sprays of molten steel would burst out
of them at any moment. Cold, heavy hail hammered at the
windows like the hard beaks of a thousand birds. The water
had no time to run down the glass and gelled in muddy patterns. In the flashes, Yegorov caught momentary glimpses of
swirling fog interwoven with thick ropes of rain, and the dim
glints of huge puddles. Their reddish, pock-marked surface
was reminiscent of cooled lava.

He shook his head and left the window.

"A nuisance," he grumbled, lying down on the hard hotel
bed.

For a while he skimmed the pages of a dog-eared adven-
ture novel, then threw the book away and returned to the
window. The lightning was still plucking out of the night
sharp images of water bubbling on the panes and the shiny
black river of asphalt below.

Yegorov fell asleep before the rain stopped. When he
awakened, it was morning. Bright glints of sunshine danced on
the walls and ceilings, reflecting endlessly from all the lac-
quered, polished, and metal objects in the room.

Yegorov stretched, jumped out of bed, and walked with

springy steps over the pleasantly cool floor. He felt fresh and energetic and full of causeless joy. Last night's rain seemed to have washed away all his fatigue and recent disappointments.

In such a mood, he thought, he would have had no difficulty in putting across his plan for exploring the Acquan Plateau and organizing the work out there. Unfortunately, it was too late—his plans had been rejected a month ago as unrealistic.

Now he was on vacation and was to spend the week resting, not working.

He expended his overflow of energy on giving his teeth a thorough brushing and dressed, humming the popular song, "I am writing to you on the Moon. . . ."

At the station, Yegorov's mood was considerably dampened.

"The helicopter will start after twelve, and the autoplane—" the cashier broke off for a moment. "That's all."

"What do you mean, 'that's all'?" Yegorov asked, examining the bald head of this relatively young man.

The cashier raised his reddish eyebrows. A glint of spite flashed through the green eyes.

"I mean just what I say—that's all," he said, bending his head to the side. "All the tickets are sold, all the seats taken. Wait, there will be a helicopter after twelve."

"I have waited here since last night."

"You're not the only one."

"But it's only forty kilometers . . ."

"We have no long-distance service. There's no one here who has to go more than a hundred kilometers."

Yegorov left the window, clenching his teeth. He stared gloomily at the other passengers. The bright sun pouring in through the glass walls cast a friendly light upon the faces of the wind- and sun-burned men, the dark-browed women in

93

colored kerchiefs, and the children playing at the feet of their parents. The low, melodic talk which filled the hall sang out with every intonation of musical Ukrainian speech.

All at once, every head turned in the same direction as though an electric current ran across the room. The flow of melodious phrases stopped; the men and women stared at a figure that appeared in the transparent revolving door.

Yegorov glanced at the door and saw a strange man. His first impression was indeterminate, but anxiety and a sense of danger swept over him.

The man was uncannily handsome. His beauty was like a challenge or the blow of a whip. Everything about him was somehow complete and perfect, yet incredibly extravagant.

The man was probably accustomed to being stared at. He walked to the ticket window as though there was no one else in the waiting room and asked with a slight foreign accent:

"They called you about me?"

The cashier's bald crown bobbed like a float on a windy day when endless ripples run over the leaden surface of the water. Yegorov could see his bony freckled hand with reddish hair where the tight cuff met the wrist. The hand rose obsequiously and with a soft movement deposited a ticket on the counter.

The man nodded, slipped the ticket into his pocket, and walked to the door. The cashier rose in his seat and called after him:

"Your auto-plane is in the third garage! On the right, as you come out. . . ."

The stranger nodded again without turning.

Yegorov went over to the window.

"So you had a free auto-plane?" he asked with deliberate calm.

The red-browed cashier continued to scribble something on his sheets, then he slowly raised his head. He looked at Yegorov with puzzled, astonished eyes. Of course, he did not recognize him.

"What auto-plane?" he asked in a tired voice.

"The one you have just given to this foreigner."

"A-a-ah," the cashier drawled, and returned to his bills.

Yegorov felt the blood rush to his head, blurring his vision like a dense brown fog.

"I am talking to you!" he banged his fist on the ledge.

The bills and receipts impaled on shiny bureaucratic spikes, the paste jar, the inkstand made of moonstone jumped in unison and dropped clicking back onto the desk. The paste jar turned over and a puddle of transparent yellowish paste crept out of it. The cashier turned pale and leaped up:

"You'll answer for this!" He pressed a button.

For a long time after that Yegorov had to wave his arms, shout, defend himself, explain himself, exhort, appeal, threaten, and flatter until at last, by nine o'clock, he set out in the stationmaster's car. Instead of a speedy, powerful auto-plane, he had to get into the antediluvian car brought from the barn of the local transportation chief.

Mentally establishing the lines of genetic kinship between the cashier and his chief, on the one hand, and animals, mainly of the canine species, on the other, Yegorov calmed down and turned his eyes to the surrounding world. It was magnificent. The blue sky high overhead, alive with wispy clouds, radiated warmth and light. The wheat, still green and fresh, sparkled with dew. A fragrance of healthy, joyous life was spread over the fields. The cool wind ruffled Yegorov's hair.

"I've been away a long time," he whispered, moved by the sight of the familiar fields and the black ribbons of roads looping around dense stands of trees.

"Musikovka?" asked the driver.

"Uh-um."

"To Nechiporenko?"

Yegorov looked at the dark, merry young man, with the strange name of Renik Reinholds.

"Yes. How did you know?"

"He has lots of visitors nowadays. Will he fly back soon?"

"He will. Give the man a chance to rest. He's just come home."

The car which had rolled easily along the highway slowed down.

"What is it?" asked Yegorov.

"We have to get off the highway here. The turn to Musikovka."

"Well, what's the problem? Turn off . . ."

"Our roads, you know, God help us! In dry weather it's not too bad, but after such a rain . . ."

The young man did not finish his sentence and turned right. The car took the sharp curve under the bridge and leaped out onto the black country road. Yegorov looked ahead with anxiety. He was familiar with the effects of rain in the black earth regions.

The road was deeply rutted. The ground under the wheels was giving way increasingly until at last the car sank up to the chassis, helplessly churning up black lumps of mud with its turning wheels.

"That's it," said Renik and stopped the motor.

They climbed out, and Yegorov sank up to his ankles into the black mud. Cursing, he pulled his foot out of the sticky mass. While he was struggling with the forces of adhesion, Renik skillfully cleared the way with a shovel.

They started and turned into another road, leading directly to Musikovka. Here the entire surface had turned into a kind of thick ooze. The car skidded every few seconds. The motor roared and black smoke poured from the exhaust pipe. Renik climbed out again, felt the radiator, and waved his hand in despair.

"We'll stop a while," he said. "Let it cool off."

Yegorov leaned against the baggage compartment and blew puffs of cigarette smoke at the mocking clear sky.

"Hell," Renik's voice spoke up beside him. "We've conquered the moon, we've conquered Mars, we've landed on Venus, but our roads are as impossible as ever. Getting to Musikovka is still harder than getting to Mars."

"The whole trouble, my dear fellow," Yegorov spoke didactically, "is that we are living in a transitional period. Auto-planes have not yet come into general use, but cars are already obsolete. When the mass production of auto-planes gets going, roads will no longer be needed. The only ones left will be superhighways, and all the rest—like this one—will be plowed under and put to crops. We'll have only handkerchief-sized landing spots for the auto-planes. And that, too, purely for tradition's sake, since an auto-plane can land anywhere—on solid ground, on water, in the woods, in swamps . . ."

"When and if . . ." Renik drawled doubtfully and returned to the driver's seat. For a long time he puttered with the starter, shifted gears, and finally announced, "Let's try to cross the field."

They turned off the road and into a field covered with the reddish stubble of last year's crop. The car leaned steeply first to the right then to the left; it was carried with astonishing ease in the most unexpected directions. The field sloped a little, and the car slithered over it like a hockey puck on ice. Renik, who had long since cut off the motor, was bearing down with all his strength upon the brakes. He stared with horror at the deep gully that cut across the field and that was steadily coming nearer. A hundred meters or so from the edge the car suddenly swerved, turned a full circle, and came to a stop.

"To hell with it," said Renik, mopping his pale face. "I'll wait till evening. Maybe the mud will dry out a bit by then."

They got out of the car.

"Musikovka is over there," Renik said, pointing across the gully.

One- and two-story houses nested on the slopes of a green, sunlit hill. Cherry trees and poplars cast delicate violet shadows on their whitewashed walls.

Yegorov said good-bye to Renik and walked along the gully toward the wooden bridge that led to the Musikovka road. His feet gradually accumulated an ever thickening coat of mud, and soon he was waddling from side to side as though on stilts and skidding as efficiently as the car. At last he swore, took off his shoes, rolled up his trousers and, clutching his muddy shoes in one hand and his briefcase in the other, squished away over the field.

"Is Vasily home?" he asked half an hour later, halting at a house which displayed a waving red flag.

A middle-aged Ukrainian woman glanced sharply at him. "And who may you be?"

"Tell him Yegorov. Sasha Yegorov."

The woman shouted through the window, and a moment later a tall young man in a T-shirt, light-colored slacks, and tennis shoes ran out to the porch. A black lock of hair curled gaily over his high forehead. His brown eyes gleamed in warm welcome.

"Sashok! Hello! Come in, come in. . . . What a sight you are! Had a taste of our black earth?"

They embraced.

"Greetings, Martian, greetings!" Yegorov said, smiling. "Couldn't stay away, could you? Ran off home!"

"I couldn't, don't you know? I stopped off at the Academy

LAST DOOR TO AIYA

straight from the cosmodrome, turned in the papers, and—
fare thee well! They wanted to shove me off to a sanatorium
but I talked them out of it. I told them I had all I needed at
home—a sanatorium, a prophylactorium, and—"

"And, of course, the maiden with a brow fair as the
moon?"

"In short, a one hundred per cent multicomponent ecologi-
cal system, assuring the astronaut the highest moral and physical well-being. Come in, come in, please."

While Yegorov was splashing under the shower, Vasily
went in and out a hundred times, now bringing a towel, now
the special Neptune soap issued only to astronauts, now
simply to say something jolly and slap Yegorov's lean back.

"In my opinion," said Yegorov, watching the black rivulets
running from his feet, "Ukrainian mud is insufficiently
reflected in the works of our classics."

"And our scientists," completed Vasily.

"Exactly. After all, they've sung about the Ukrainian night,
the wide and mighty Dnieper, the Ukrainian girls, and even
your sycamores. Why are there no voluminous studies or
inspired poems about the dark powers that come into their
own hereabouts after rains?"

"In fact, there is a lack of competent scientific dissertation
on this matter. A fertile subject for a dozen candidate's theses
and two or three doctoral dissertations is going to waste!"

"I'll say," Yegorov laughed. "Mud can be classified
according to the date of origin: antique mud . . ."

"And according to the traction energy required to pull
one's foot out of it."

"Light mud—one kilogram; heavy mud—half a ton . . ."

"The figures cited by the author of the thesis characterizing
heavy mud seem to be somewhat exaggerated. Our experiments have given lower results, but this, of course, in no way
reflects on the merits of the work, and the author is unques-

tionably . . ." Vasily droned on, bending over the imaginary
pages of the examiner's comments on the imaginary dissertation.

". . . unquestionably deserves to be granted the degree of
Candidate of Muddy Science!" Yegorov completed.

Vasily solemnly pressed his hand.

"You will live in the attic with me, all right? I'd give you a
separate room but I have another guest. He flew in today."

"Who?"

"Tend, he was in the Disney group. We worked together on
Mars."

"Oh! And where is he from?"

"South America."

Yegorov raised his eyebrows.

"What the devil does he want with you?"

"I'll tell you later," Vasily answered. "Come, I'll introduce
you to the family."

The family turned out to consist of two persons: Vasily's
mother, the middle-aged Ukrainian woman with the suspicious
glance, and his sister, a tall young woman with mischievous
dark eyes, very much like her brother's. She pressed Yegorov's
hand and said, smiling:

"Vasya has spoken a lot about you. . . ."

"Really? What did he say?"

"Oh, well . . ." the girl squinted slyly.

"Oxana, don't bother Sasha. You'd better run over to the
store," Vasily interrupted her.

"And where is your South American?" asked Yegorov
when they climbed the stairs to Vasily's room.

"Sleeping," the astronaut answered, stretching. "The
minute he came he went to sleep."

Yegorov looked enviously at Vasily. An athlete's strength
and invincible health were expressed in every movement of his
magnificent body.

100

"Shall we talk?"

"After lunch. I must help mother in the house first. It's hard for her now, alone with Oxana, without a man around."

"Go on. And call me if you need me."

Vasily went downstairs. Alone, Yegorov looked about him. It was a strange room. Judging from the furniture and the various objects it contained, someone had very boldly combined within it elements of a laboratory, library, cosmic museum, living room, and bedroom. The latter, however, was represented only by a narrow bed covered with a plain woolen blanket. Over the bed hung four photographs of Vasily: one, as a schoolboy, a mop-headed, pugnacious brat, staring intently into the camera, and three space shots, all of them made on the moon. Strange, none from Mars. Yet he was there five times, thought Yegorov.

He stroked the expensive bindings of books on cosmonautics which occupied an entire wall, snapped his finger on the gray moonstone that looked like the petrified crest of a wave, smiled at the model of the navigation panel of a space ship. He knew this piece very well. Vasily had built it when they were both students at the Institute of Cosmic Geology. Then he walked to the wide glass door leading to the balcony. He pushed the door and stepped out onto a large terrace, open on three sides and protected from direct sun rays above by strips of silk awning.

Yegorov saw the village—the fresh, dark-green trees, the pleasant little houses with whitewashed walls, the towers with auto-planes, their yellow and scarlet sides gleaming in the sun. From somewhere came the crowing of a rooster, the lowing of a cow. A blue haze hung over Musikovka, promising a hot afternoon.

Yegorov inhaled deeply of the heady air, holding the fragrance of thousands of grasses and flowers. The bright light and glitter made him slightly dizzy. He thought that in

Moscow he would be sitting now in a smoke-filled, stuffy room, feeding "Big Beta" endless columns of figures drawn from the data of geological prospecting expeditions to the moon and Mars. And waiting nervously while the clever machine was preparing the answer that would either confirm or refute his hypothesis, his ability to forecast. Then would come the evening. Swimming in the pool or sitting at the bar "The Crater," he would try to drive out the fatigue that permeated his body and his brain cells, to relax his overtaxed nerves. And the next day everything would start again. The soul-draining work, the failures, the miscalculations. And the occasional successes that one neither enjoys nor even notices. . . . And all the time, while his life was being spent at the console of a computer, this tender, joyous sun was shining, these sweet breezes sang, welcoming the day.

A noise reached his ears. Someone had entered the room. Yegorov saw the man's reflection in the glass.

"Vasily!" a low voice said.

Something checked Yegorov and he remained silent. He recognized the man on the threshold. The handsome foreigner who had gotten the auto-plane at the station.

Yegorov saw his face clearly. It was tense and listening. Hearing no answer, the stranger cautiously stepped into the room. Or, rather, seeped into it, so soft and noiseless was his movement. He closed the door behind him. Then he stopped in the middle of the room, searching the walls with his eyes.

"Vasily!"

Yegorov was just about to leave his hiding place when Vasily came in.

"A-ah! Angelo!" he said. "Have you rested?"

"Oh! Excellently. Very."

"Good. Let's go down."

They left and Yegorov moved into the room.

That pretty boy, thought Yegorov, is most unsympathetic. He decided to question Vasily about him, but no opportunity presented itself before lunch.

Nechiporenko would appear in the door for a moment with a worried air and disappear immediately. Yegorov heard now the grating talk of the old woman, and now Oxana's fresh, ringing voice.

"Vasil, come here! Vasil! Where are you, Vasil?"

Vasily obediently tramped over the amber-yellow floor at the beck and call of his family.

At lunch there was a new guest, a moustached old man. His name was Pavich. He was self-satisfied, pompous, and boastful.

"To our dear neighbor, the world-famous astronaut Nechiporenko!" proclaimed Pavich, raising his glass. Drinking down, he grunted and wiped his moustache.

Then the old man expatiated in popular terms for the benefit of all present on Vasily's services to his homeland and humanity. Vasily made faces but did not interrupt the guest.

"That'll do, grandpa," Vasily's mother, Olga Panteleyevna, finally broke in. "We read the papers, too."

"That's all right, Olga, that's all right. We've got a single astronaut here for the whole region. And from our village, too! Such marvels should be celebrated."

"Well, celebrate all you want. But don't keep telling us what everybody knows."

Yegorov watched the South American from the corner of his eye. Angelo Tend kept putting away one well-browned potato after another with an air of utmost indifference. He seemed even more dazzling than that morning at the station. A delicate, peach-colored flush played on his clear white skin. The huge black eyes were severe and faintly melancholy. He obviously charmed Oxana. The girl sat without raising her eyes from the plate. When she was addressed, she would start. Where was her sly, playful smile? Yegorov noted the girl's condition with regret, and thought to himself, Women!

"What's fame?" Olga Panteleyevna said angrily, and her face now seemed open and sad. "The important thing is health. Take Grisha Rogozhin, Vasya's comrade . . ."

"Mother!"

"I'm not saying a thing. But I will tell you, Vasya, every time you go up into your cosmos, my heart sinks."

"Naturally—a mother's heart," Pavich pronounced, stroking the yellowed ends of his moustache and tasting the fried bream.

"If father were alive, he'd get gray hairs from Vasya's flights."

"We must, mother, we must," Vasily spoke firmly.

"I'm not saying anything. If you must, you must. But why shouldn't you take a rest? Go abroad, see the world."

"Abroad! What's that to him?" Pavich winked slyly. "He's got a firm anchor right here in Musikovka."

"A fine anchor!" Olga Panteleyevna collected the dishes and angrily sailed out of the room.

"Mama, it seems, does not approve of your girl, Vasily, eh?" Pavich burst out laughing and dipped his potato in cream.

Yegorov saw that this conversation was unpleasant for Vasily. He turned to Oxana.

"And you, Oxana, are you planning a trip to Mars?"

"Uh," the girl flushed, "who needs your bugs!"

"Those bugs are cleverer than all of us," Vasily remarked.

"Maybe so. But they're all dead."

"Say, Vasyatka," the old man fidgeted gaily. "Instead of flying off to Mars, why not visit our own anthill?"

"Right," Olga Panteleyevna approved as she returned. "There are plenty of dead ants on earth."

Angelo Tend put down his fork.

"There is as much resemblance between a Martian and an ant as between a man and a kitten. A great civilization was developed on Mars. Earth won't reach its level for another ten thousand years. And the Martians are not extinct."

He looked sternly at Oxana. His eyes burned with the fierce flame of some unknown dark faith.

"Where are they, then?" the girl asked timidly.

"They went away to Aiya."

Everyone was silent.

"And what's that?" Pavich asked mockingly.

"We don't know," Vasily answered for Angelo. "There is much we do not understand about the civilization of the Martians. They did not know verbal or sound communication; the logic of their thinking was qualitatively different from ours. Their evolution took very different channels. Their methods of production and the development of their society are still unclear to us."

"If we ever come to understand all the objects found on Mars, our own society will take a great step forward," said Yegorov.

Angelo looked directly at him for the first time.

What an eerie feeling. He seems to be sucking something out of me, thought the geologist, involuntarily dropping his eyes.

"Yes, you are quite right," said Tend. There was something metallic in his voice.

No overtones, thought Yegorov.

"Well, all that is for the Academy of Sciences," said Pavich. "But for people, there's nothing there to put your hands on, to . . ." the old man waved his gnarled thick fingers, unable to find words to express his thought.

"Nothing to slip inside your coat and take home?" smiled Vasily.

"Oh . . . I mean . . . that's not what I mean, lad! I mean, something like ores or metals of some kind."

"Sure, sure," Olga Panteleyevna broke in. "Why, Vasya's room is full of rocks."

Vasily laughed.

"You aren't right, mama," Oxana said slyly. "What about the mirror?"

"What mirror?" asked Yegorov.

"Vasya brought me a present—a mirror from Mars."

"A lid from a Martian vanity chest," Olga Panteleyevna mocked. "Doesn't even have a hook so you might hang it up."

"But then, it doesn't get dusty," remarked Vasily.

Angelo glanced at Oxana. He seemed to see her for the first time.

"And how do you like looking into it?" he asked.

"Very much," smiled the girl.

"Let us drink to Mother Earth," Pavich proclaimed solemnly. "It made us, it nurtured us, and it sent us off into the cosmos."

After lunch Vasily said to Yegorov:

"Come, let's bring your bed upstairs."

"Where is it?"

"In Oxana's room."

He turned to his sister, who was engaged in a lively conversation with Angelo.

"Oxana, we'll take the divan from your room, all right?"

"Certainly, do," said the girl, without turning her head.

Oxana's room was clean and spacious, filled with the fine aroma of wild flowers.

Suddenly Yegorov caught sight of the mirror from Mars. It stood on a chair, leaning against its back. Oxana had thrown a towel over the top of it.

"Is this it?" Yegorov asked, approaching the mirror.

The surface of the half-meter-long oval, held in a thick,

golden-gray frame, reflected in its depths the intent gray eyes of the young man. The mirror did not distort a single line of his face but lent the reflection a faint bluish tinge. Yegorov felt as though he were looking through a thick layer of blue water.

Vasily, who was also looking into the mirror, said suddenly to Oxana, who had followed them into the room, "Look, sister, lend us this thing for a while, eh? We both have to shave in the morning, and I have only my little traveling mirror left."

"Take it. And, by the way, you can use both sides. Hang it in the middle of the room and you can shave at the same time."

"We'll do just that."

They brought the divan upstairs, and took along the mirror.

"I'll sleep on the terrace," said Yegorov.

"Fine," Vasily agreed.

The divan was placed under the awning. From it, Yegorov could see the whole of Musikovka and the blue vistas of the steppes beyond. They hung the mirror nearby, wrapping insulating tape around the golden rim, and attaching the end of the tape to the rack on which the silk awning was stretched. The mirror swayed and glittered in the sun.

"It's heavy," remarked Yegorov, casting an appraising glance at the results of their labors.

"Very. And I wonder why. We've turned over nearly two thousand of them to the Academy. All the chemists of the world are struggling to discover their composition."

They went to Vasily's study, for the terrace was becoming too hot.

"Generally, the Martians had a strange predilection for elliptical shapes," said Vasily when they sat down in the deep, cool armchairs. "They had tens of thousands of mirrors like

107

this one; in their cities the mirrors served as reflectors of light. Many buildings on Mars are elliptic in shape."

Vasily fell silent. An image of the Large Martian Capital rose before his eyes. He shook his head.

"All right," he said. "We'll talk about me later. But you probably know everything from the reports sent in to your Institute. How do you like working there?"

Yegorov reflected for a moment.

"How shall I put it? I do, but not quite, as we used to say in Odessa. When I failed to make the space team after graduation because of my liver . . . Well, you remember. Of course, it's lucky I am a geologist, not a navigator like you. That would have been the end of me altogether. Still, I couldn't give up space. The Institute was the next best thing. I worked. I studied the data collected on Mars, and discovered the Acquan Plateau. Now I cling to the hope that we'll be able to carry out some studies there."

"Officially? Don't think of it," said Vasily. "The conditions there are terrible. Six of us excavated the Large Capital. Imagine, a billion Martians lived there once upon a time. It goes about three or four hundred meters down into the ground, and its surface area has not yet been determined. For two months we crawled about those damned anthill passages without taking off our space suits. You finish your shift, and you can barely crawl back to 'Moscow.' That's how it was. But tell me about your plateau."

Yegorov scratched his chin. He looked up at the ceiling, and began:

"You remember the excitement when elements unknown on earth were discovered on Mars? The laboratories could not synthesize them, no matter how they tried. On Mars, they are concentrated in one place, and in huge quantities. I've named this place the Acquan Plateau. Later we succeeded in proving the artificial origin of these elements. And what do you think this means?"

108

"Well, the by-products of thermonuclear reactions—" Vasily said tentatively.

"Right. The by-products. This is very important. The Martians, who built their civilization underground, utilized the surface of Mars just as we once utilized the upper layers of the atmosphere and the ocean bottom. They threw all sorts of refuse to the surface. Actually, those were the signs that led to the discovery of the Large Underground Capital and the entire branching system of their cities."

"So you think that under the Acquan Plateau there is a thermonuclear energy center which nobody has found as yet?"

"Quite. And if this center is found, I believe that we shall be able to draw some useful lessons from it. Especially in view of the level of Martian technology. You see?"

"It's an interesting and important question. But finding it is not all. We must learn to understand how they did things. Here we've discovered the first extraterrestrial civilization, and what's the good of it? Oh, well. What do your chiefs say?"

"First, the plateau is enormous. Second, the center may turn out to be not under the plateau, but somewhere nearby. The expenses would be too high. Third, it is easier to study and bring back already discovered objects than to look for new ones. In short, it's something for the future."

"Yes, the situation isn't easy," Vasily said reflectively. "But it's worth looking into. However, you understand, without official say-so . . . It's a risk. The instructions say that we must weigh and measure every move four times over. And even then—"

He fell silent.

"You understand, Sasha," Nechiporenko finally brought out with an effort. "Mars is a very strange planet. I know our moon very well, I took part in the landing on Venus and had a taste of its gases, but all of it is something else. Something else altogether. Both on the moon and on Venus you have dangerous conditions, raging storms, and so on. But you aren't

109

frightened. On Mars it is sometimes very frightening. Do you understand?"

Yegorov looked at him with astonishment.

"Yes, yes," Vasily said with agitation. "No one writes about it, and people don't even like to talk about it, but it is so."

He was silent again.

"Mars is an amazingly calm planet. Fairly level surface. Giant cities concealed deep underground. Dead cities. Not a single Martian is left; we found only billions of strange dry shells. Perhaps the chitin coating of insects, or some sort of clothing. Before departure to Aiya, they either abandoned these shells, or—and here we're up against sheer guesswork. Up to now we've not been able to establish anything with certainty. The Martians built giant constructions underground, which make men feel like Lilliputians. What ends these constructions served we can only conjecture. It is very difficult to work there, Sasha. You are forever haunted by the feeling that there is someone on this dead planet."

"What nonsense—" Yegorov drawled.

"Oh, yes, yes, don't smile. You constantly feel as though somebody alive were right behind you, watching and taking stock of you. And waiting. I don't know anything more terrifying than this sensation of expectancy. Something is constantly waiting for you there. It's a most unpleasant feeling."

"Must be!"

"Now take our wretched efforts to decode the incomprehensible visual-tactile information that is recorded on the crystals of the Red Cupola. The only interesting conclusion we came to is that the Martians were preparing to leave for Aiya. But what is Aiya? And how were two billion Martians transported there? It's beyond comprehension. And who will tell us why all the information refers only to the last decade of the Martian civilization? Where are their archives? Did they have libraries? In a word—a million riddles."

"I don't understand why you are so upset. The study of this complex society, so different from ours, naturally must take time."

"It's not a question of time, Sasha. I suspect that there are many things we'll never understand."

"Details, perhaps. Details are always unique and elusive. But we'll surely learn to understand the general framework."

"Not even that. I was told that the Disneys—they worked on the decoding of the crystals of the Eastern sector of the Red Cupola—have reached interesting conclusions. They say that the thinking of the Martians is, in a way, the opposite, the reverse of ours. Here on earth, motion is a property of matter; there, matter is a property of motion—its manifestation."

"I must catch you here," said Yegorov. "In order to draw such a conclusion about the character of Martian thinking, it is necessary to command a vast store of information. Why, this is a philosophic generalization!"

"No. The Disneys had no more information than we have. Our discoveries duplicate one another. But they were luckier. You see, Sasha, I have the feeling—" He became thoughtful. Mentally, he saw the narrow deep well down which the elevator was taking the cosmo-geologists to the Large Capital; he saw the endless labyrinth of passages that could be traversed only by crawling, and the Red Cupola—the huge artificial cave with an oval ceiling bathed in scarlet light. And once again he was gripped by the familiar feeling of anxious expectation.

"I have a feeling, Sasha," Vasily continued, "that somebody is controlling and directing our finds and our discoveries on Mars."

"Of course. The Academy of Sciences, the Council on—"

"No," Vasily interrupted him. "That's not what I mean. I am not talking about our people."

Yegorov pretended not to understand his friend. He turned away and looked out at the terrace.

111

"Yes," said Vasily. "Someone is directing us, putting one thing in our way, hiding others for the time being. In short, controlling us. Judge for yourself—the Martians left for Aiya about five million years ago. At that time there were still no men on earth. Yet the Martian cities are preserved like new; everything glitters there. This is unnatural, don't you see? There is a second law of thermodynamics, there is such a thing as progressive entropy. Why, the place should be in a chaotic shambles after five million years! But there is no chaos! There is strict order."

"What are you leading up to?"

Vasily silently bent closer to Yegorov. The other looked with alarm into his serious black eyes. Had he lost his mind on Mars? The thought flicked like a lizard through Yegorov's brain.

"They will return."

Yegorov answered with a forced laugh, "A fine theory! The master has gone out for a minute and asks the guests to wait?"

"Not at all. The master simply cannot, or does not, want to come back."

"Perhaps they left the solar system to go to this Aiya?"

"The devil knows what this Aiya is," Vasily said pensively. "At times I am even ready to agree with Academician Perov. He investigated the armor, and he thinks that the 'migration' is nothing but a physiological process. Aiya, according to him, means death. Or perhaps it's the other world. By going off to Aiya, you get a chance for immortality."

"Is that your own addition to the theory?"

"No, the Disneys thought so. Incidentally, this Angelo Tend—not a bad fellow, by the way—worked with them until our arrival. The Disneys were all ready to leave when they discovered that Tend had disappeared. They looked for him here and there, but no Angelo. A month later we found Tend in

112

one of the galleries of the Red Cupola. He was quite well, but he could not answer a single question. He did not remember what had happened to him, where he had been, what he had eaten or drunk. We had to teach him everything all over again. He had to be told who he was, where he lived, and even that there was an earth and people. This went on for a long time. But one day he remembered almost everything."

Vasily's words were interrupted by a shrill sound that seemed to rend the air. The piercing whine rose to the sky like a column. The friends ran out on the balcony. Above them, a jet plane was tracing a snowy signature on the dark-blue expanse of sky.

"Looks like a new model," said Yegorov, shielding his eyes with his hand.

The sound broke off as suddenly as it began. The plane vanished in the depths of the blue.

"What a roarer!" Vasily shook his head. "By the time it reaches the ground, the sound is reduced. Can you imagine how it is for the fliers?"

"They've soundproofing."

"What was I talking about?" asked Vasily.

"Angelo."

"Oh, yes! Well, actually that was all. Since we returned from Mars, Angelo has been home but he did not like it there. He's a Spaniard, you know, from Venezuela. Now he's decided to stay with us."

"And this mirror that I brought for Oxana," continued Vasily, "is a memento from Grishka Rogozhin, who died . . ."

"What?" Yegorov jumped up. "Grigory is dead?"

"He died, and under the most mysterious circumstances. He worked in one of the innumerable 'cells' in the Red Cupola, and our blasting team worked on the floor above. The explosion was tiny; still, there must have been a bit of a shock. There was a cry. We came running to Grisha and found him

113

with a smashed skull. His helmet was off, his face crushed. But the 'cell' where he had been working was absolutely undamaged. There was only some dust from the ceiling and a few tiny pieces of plaster as big as my nail on the floor. We never learned what it was that could have dealt him such a smashing blow. They talked about multiple amplification of the blast wave, about guided impact—but that's nonsense. And what a shame it was! Just that day Grisha had made a magnificent discovery. He found a Martian's corpse. It was a most marvelous find. In five years on Mars we found nothing but empty shells. Billions of those damned lobster skins! We could only guess about the real appearance of the Martians. Grishka created a sensation when he dragged in that beautifully dried-out specimen under his arm. We put it in a titanium container and sent it up. And four hours later we had to send Grisha up as well. I kept the mirror." Vasily pointed at the mirror from Mars. It swayed lightly under the gusts of warm wind. "The dead Martian lay two steps away from it. Grigory had taken it down. I took the mirror as a memento."

Yegorov glanced sadly and attentively at the gleaming oval.

"And that's another riddle," Vasily said slowly. "Why did the Martians need these mirrors, all of them the same, and in such vast numbers? There are hundreds of them in every city . . ."

Suddenly his face changed. He rose in his seat, supporting himself on his hands. His eyes stared at the mirror. "It does not reflect!" he whispered.

Yegorov looked at the mirror. At first glance, it really seemed to reflect nothing. Its surface was even and opaque, and of the same golden-gray color as the rim. They rushed toward it together and saw their excited faces in it.

"Whew, what idiocy," said Yegorov. "Anisotropic reflection, that's all. You've made me so nervous with your stories about Mars that I'm ready to shy away from any piece of Martian rock."

"You'll do well to," Vasily said thoughtfully. "None of the Martion mirrors I saw possessed such properties. Neither did this one, while it remained in my suitcase."

"It must have been affected by my arrival," Yegorov joked.

"Perhaps . . . Oh, well," said Vasily, "To sum up, we may say that, although Mars is a dangerous planet, the Acquan Plateau should be explored."

"Ah, if they would take me into space!" Yegorov waved his fist.

"Don't worry about it," said Vasily. "Soon they'll build an antigravitator, and you'll be able to fly despite your bad liver. And if you don't, it won't be a great misfortune either. You'll go to some nice warm spa to drink mineral water."

Vasily left, and Yegorov walked up to the mirror. He imagined the thousands of Martians who had looked into that shiny surface, and it gave him an eerie feeling. The mirror indifferently reflected Yegorov's homely face, the red roofs of the houses, the wide green field and the electric tractor that hummed away at its far end. Suddenly it seemed to Yegorov that a faintly visible whitish film had spread over the shiny material. He touched it and recoiled in shock. The surface of the mirror was soft! He took a match and tried to scrape off film. The match made a small shallow cut across the reflection of the fiield. Yegorov was astonished. He looked at the tip of the match. Gradually, the trace of the match on the mirror began to close up and after five minutes it disappeared.

"Interesting," Yegorov mumbled and moved his chair nearer.

"Sasha! Sasha!" he heard Vasily's loud cry.

Yegorov looked down and saw Vasily standing at the gate and waving a newspaper. His face was twisted in a painful grimace.

"Jump down here!" he cried.

Yegorov jumped onto the moist resilient earth. In the bright summer sun, Vasily's face was somber and serious.

"Read this," he said, pointing to the second column.

"It is reported . . ." muttered Yegorov, skimming the small print, "that the bodies of the well-known cosmologists, the brothers Alfred, William, Calder, and James Disney were found yesterday in Boston . . . the murderer has not been found . . . Mysterious death without any signs of physical violence or toxic condition . . . Experts and scientists at a loss. . . . What does this mean?" he turned to Vasily.

"Read to the end," Vasily said angrily.

"The deaths of the famous explorers of Mars are linked to the announcement they had issued several days before, stating that an archive had been found in the Great Martian Capital, along with a key to it, making it possible to recreate the so-called door to Aiya. This discovery will immeasurably increase the scope of human knowledge, according to Calder Disney's statement to the *Times* correspondents."

They looked at one another silently.

"That's Mars for you!" the astronaut said in agitation. "It stretches its paws even to earth. The Martians don't want their secrets revealed."

Yegorov was silent, but the report alarmed him, too. He recalled that Angelo had just returned from America and probably knew about the Disneys' deaths.

"It may well be that one fine day the body of Vasily Nechiporenko will be found without traces of any physical, chemical, or psychic violence," the astronaut said suddenly, examining the daffodils that edged the flowerbed in front of the house.

Yegorov glanced at the print of his foot at the edge of the bed and asked:

"And what does your Angelo say about it?"

"He does not know yet. I'll call him now."

Vasily went into the house and came out with Tend a moment later.

Neither agitation, nor sympathy, nor regret—nothing was reflected in Angelo's handsome face. "He is thinking over his course of action," Yegorov thought suddenly.

"What sad news. I respected them a great deal," Tend said quietly.

His face remained immobile. Perhaps this is his usual expression, or, rather, total lack of any expression, thought Yegorov.

They sat down on the bench by the gate. Oxana was cutting some narcissi nearby.

"The strangest thing is that the people who worked in the Red Cupola seem to be picked for death. Grisha Rogozhin, the Disneys. I wonder who is next?"

"I," Angelo said suddenly and smiled.

This was the first time Yegorov had seen Tend smile: his eyes remained deadly calm, and the mouth twisted in a paroxysm of laughter.

"Why do you think so?" asked Vasily.

"If we are to follow your theory that the Martians are hiding their secrets from us, it must be I. The Disneys deciphered the archive, and they died; Grisha found the mummy, and he died. And I . . . before I . . . before I suffered that lapse of memory I also saw the room where Grisha had been found. I saw the mummified Martian, and the mirror, and a number of little crosses on the walls and ceiling."

"What little crosses?"

"How do I know? I came there with a flashlight but it went out of order. Then I took the two ends of the battery and with the graphite holder made a small voltaic arc. I saw this Martian on the floor, the mirror, and flashes on the wall and ceiling that looked like crosses. At that point my arc flared up—I had probably brought the electrodes too close."

Angelo spoke somehow reluctantly, as though something were holding him back.

"And then?"

"There was a noise. A very loud noise, like the roaring of a plane at take-off. The arc went out, and the noise stopped. I got out of the room and lost my way in the passages. According to my calculations, about two hours went by. But when I met your people, Vasya, they told me that I had been gone a month and that Calder's group had already completed its work and returned to earth."

There was a long silence. Oxana walked by and threw a flower into each man's lap.

"And did you go to that room again?" Yegorov asked Tend.

"Yes. I found no crosses there."

"Well, my friends," said Vasily, getting up. "I must go now. It will not do to pay too much attention to Martian affairs on earth. Valya is waiting for me. . . ."

Yegorov returned to the balcony. Oxana and Angelo remained in the garden and they were talking quietly. Yegorov lay down on the sofa and, inclining the mirror toward himself, began to watch Oxana. It seemed to him that Angelo leaned a little too intimately toward her. Yegorov threw the narcissus at the mirror. He could not understand himself why he had done it.

There was a scream from behind him. The astonished Yegorov let the mirror swing back and turned. Angelo and Oxana had fallen off the bench into the flowers. They floundered clumsily, trying to get up. Yegorov jumped down from the balcony.

The second jump in one morning; it is becoming my regular method of locomotion, he thought, helping the girl and Tend to rise to their feet.

"What happened?" asked Yegorov.

Oxana's face was startled and confused. There was a red gash on her cheek. Yegorov smelled a sharp unpleasant odor in the air.

"Something pushed us," Angelo said after a moment's thought. "As though a cloud dropped on us. A cloud of smell. And it vanished instantly."

"No, not a cloud—it felt as if a ceiling had fallen on us, with all the plaster. And that strange smell . . . like garbage, like something putrid," said Oxana.

"You are not hurt?"

She shook her head. Yegorov looked around. He saw nothing extraordinary except the trampled flowerbed.

The smell was gradually dissipating. At first sharp and nauseating, it grew fainter and more delicate. The concentration is decreasing, Yegorov thought. He knew that even the best perfumes smell vile in strong concentration. Inhaling the delicate, elusive fragrance, he tried to define it. "Narcissi" it suddenly dawned on him.

He glanced at the balcony. A vague guess flashed in his mind. Yegorov looked at Angelo and saw that he too was gazing at the balcony, at the extraordinary mirror. Yegorov was struck with the expression on the young scientist's face: it was the expression of a man looking at an object of cherished and long-concealed desire.

"Isn't the mirror in your room?" Tend asked Oxana in a breaking voice.

"The mirror? What mirror? Ah, that one! I gave it to Sasha and Vasily," the girl answered casually and with slight surprise. She had also noticed Tend's agitation.

Something is wrong here, thought Yegorov.

He was distracted by a noise at the gates.

119

Olga Panteleyevna and Pavich came into the yard. She was wearing rubber boots and a leather jacket and spoke angrily to Pavich:

"And I tell you he was drunk, you understand, drunk!"

Pavich held an old frayed briefcase with a metal lock in one hand, and a yard-long piece of wood in the other.

"But here's material evidence, Olga," Pavich said, swinging the log.

"What happened, Mother?" asked Oxana, approaching them.

After running the obstacle race of numerous digressions and exclamations, Oxana and Yegorov at last managed to obtain an explanation. Olga Panteleyevna had gone with Pavich to examine the fields and discovered a deep furrow across the field of winter wheat. The broken shoots and upturned soil had led them to the tractor driver Kotzubenko who was sitting nearby and staring in amazement at the ditch across the smooth green field. In reply to questions, he babbled incomprehensible nonsense. He insisted that a huge beam had fallen from the sky and gone across the field by itself, leaving a deep rut. The piece of wood in Pavich's hand was a fragment of the beam.

At first, Kotzubenko had said, the trench had been about three meters deep. Then it began to diminish, as though closing up, the wheat straightened up, and by the time Olga Panteleyevna and Pavich had come, it was no more than a small furrow, which they had thought was the track of the tractor. The action of the drunken tractor driver—and he was really drunk—provoked Olga Panteleyevna to violent indignation.

Yegorov wondered. Then he noticed that Angelo was no longer with them. He must have withdrawn when no one was looking.

Opening the door to Vasily's study, Yegorov felt that he

would find the Spaniard there. But there was no one in the room. He went out on the balcony. Tend was standing with his back to Yegorov, holding a slender black rod to the golden-gray frame of the mirror. Angelo's ear was bent to the other end of the rod, as though he were listening to a sick man's heart. A low hum spread in the warm spring air.

"Angelo!" Yegorov called.

Tend jumped away from the mirror, as if something had stung him. He looked into Yegorov's eyes. It was a terrifying, merciless look. . . .

Oxana stepped into Vasily's room, hearing a faint moan. It came from behind the glass door of the balcony. The girl ran out and found Yegorov on the floor, behind the boxes of seedlings and flowers. She helped him to the sofa. A few minutes later Yegorov opened his eyes.

"Is he gone?"

"Who?"

Yegorov did not answer. He looked at Oxana with weary and indifferent eyes.

"What is the matter with you?" Oxana asked anxiously. "Shall I call a doctor?"

"A doctor?" asked Yegorov. "No, there is no need for a doctor. I am perfectly well. It's the sun. I have not been out in the sun so much for a long time." He carefully studied his hands. "Oxana, with the exception of Vasily, you have spoken to Angelo more than anyone else. What do you think of him?"

The girl blushed faintly.

"I don't know, he is handsome. . . ."

"And that's all?"

"It seems to me that he is a very cold man and difficult to understand."

Yegorov smiled suddenly and sat up on the sofa.

"Your feelings are right, Oxana. Now, listen, I must see Vasily at once. Where is he?"

"He has taken Valya up in his auto-plane. If you had called in the morning, you needn't have trudged through the mud."

"How was I to know that Vasily has a personal auto-plane? Does he have a telephone in it by any chance?"

"He does. But is it important enough to disturb him? They are having a difficult time as it is. Mamma does not approve of Valya. It seems to her that Vasily needs a different wife."

Yegorov thought for a moment.

"Oxana, dear, I need Vasily most urgently. How can I call him?"

"There they are!" Oxana pointed to the horizon.

"Where? Where?" Yegorov tried to find the shiny dot over the field.

"Your eyes are strained from too much sun," remarked Oxana and, turning Yegorov by the shoulders, said: "Look in the mirror. You can see them here too. You see, this bright dot?"

"Where?"

"Oh, heavens, right here!" Oxana poked her finger into the mirror.

"Careful!" cried Yegorov, catching her hand.

But it was too late. The sunburned finger had already touched the mirror lightly on the bright spot of the reflected auto-plane. Oxana turned pale and recoiled.

"Oh!" she cried, shaking her hand. A drop of blood appeared on her finger, and the skin was slightly grazed.

"Get a car, quick!" Yegorov hurried. "Something's happened to them!"

He ran over to the balcony railing and jumped down. The third time . . . he thought mechanically.

"Oxana!" he cried, turning to the balcony. "Cover the mirror and see that no one touches it!"

The young woman, her fingers in her mouth, watched

122

Yegorov's hurried movements with astonishment. He jumped on a motorcycle. His anxiety infected her, too. She looked up at the horizon. Vasily's auto-plane was not there.

When Yegorov's motorcycle, bouncing over the dried lumps of earth, drew up to the place of the accident, a car was already there. The local agronomist had seen the plane fall. He had just emerged from his car and was walking across the field. Yegorov caught up with him and they strode on together.

A few moments later they stopped near the auto-plane, which was lying on the freshly plowed earth. Its radiator and the top of its transparent body were covered by strips of some dirty-yellow fabric stained with congealing blood. The sides and the windows of the auto-plane were splashed with small red spots. Trying to master his horror, Yegorov rushed to the machine and flung open the door.

Vasily, who was sitting at the controls, tumbled out at his feet. Together with the agronomist, Yegorov picked up the astronaut's body, which had suddenly become extraordinarily heavy, and placed him on the black soil. Then they carried out the tall pale girl, whose blue unseeing eyes were slightly open.

The agronomist opened the astronaut's collar and laid his ear to his chest.

You were right, Vasya, thought Yegorov, staring at his friend's bluish-pale face. Mars has long hands. . . .

"It's beating!" the agronomist cried with relief.

He kneeled at Vasily's head and began the rhythmic movements of artificial respiration.

Yegorov busied himself with the girl.

But why so much blood? the geologist strained to understand. They don't have a single scratch. Suddenly he recalled the ruby drop on Oxana's finger and shook his head, driving away the wild, absurd idea. A faint sigh came from Valya's lips.

123

"Valya! Valya!" called Yegorov.

"Look!" exclaimed the agronomist.

Yegorov looked up at him and saw a brick-red face, astonished blue eyes in a network of wrinkles, and a sunburned hand pointing at the auto-plane.

Neither the drops of blood on the glass, nor the steaming puddle of blood under the auto-plane were there any longer. Everything had vanished. Only a small wisp of the shriveled fabric which had a moment ago covered the entire craft was still faintly visible on the hood.

"The devil!" cried Yegorov and ran to the auto-plane. He peeled off the wisp and put it in his pocket; it was damp and cold.

Vasily opened his eyes and moaned.

"Valya!" he called quietly.

The fuss around the astronaut and his fiancée, the doctor's visit, and lengthy explanations and conversations with members of the family occupied the rest of the day. Finally, Vasily was put to bed, in spite of his loud protests, and given tea with raspberry jam, the standard remedy for all ills. Resting on a pile of pillows, he rolled his eyes and called upon all the constellations of the universe to bear witness to the fact that he was well, uninjured, and had no desire whatsoever to stay in bed. But his mother and Oxana, sitting on either side of his bed, were implacable.

"But, heavens, you must understand that nothing dreadful has happened! The auto-plane was only two or three meters above the field. Then something seemed to hit us and we lost consciousness. That's all. And there's no need to keep me in bed, according to the latest word in cosmic medicine."

"I've told you, over my dead body," Olga Panteleyevna said, pressing her son's shoulder back into the pillows with her small dry fist. "Lie still."

Oxana and Yegorov exchanged glances and burst out

laughing. Yegorov went up to his balcony. He felt exhausted. The sun had already set, but the sky was bright crimson. The village was hidden in deep shadows.

Yegorov took out the wisp of unfamiliar fabric he had taken from the auto-plane. It had become still smaller. He smoothed it out and held it up to the light. It was faintly translucent.

"Skin! Human skin! Skin from Oxana's finger," he said quietly.

Vasily was already dozing on the down pillows when someone insistently plucked him by the hand. In the shimmering moonlight he saw the figure of his friend. Yegorov was pressing his fingers to his lips.

"Sh-sh," said Yegorov. "Can you come?"

"Yes. What happened?" asked Vasily, jumping up. "anything wrong with Valya?"

"No, Valya is perfectly all right. Come with me."

Yegorov walked ahead, carefully lifting his feet. The house was silent. An orange strip of light glowed under the door of Olga Panteleyevna's room.

Yegorov brought Vasily to the study on the second floor, where a stranger sat in the dim light of the desk lamp.

"Captain Samoylenko," he introduced himself, rising.

Vasily pressed the extended hand.

"This comrade has come to arrest Tend," said Yegorov. "Angelo killed the Disneys, stole their materials and escaped."

"What?" Vasily straightened up. "Do you understand what you are saying?"

"I do. Time is short. The comrade was lucky he met me first. Tend is a dangerous criminal."

"The Americans have asked us to arrest the murderer of the four famous Mars explorers," said Samoylenko.

"But why would he do it?" cried Vasily.

"Power, gold. . . . Who knows why?" said Yegorov.

"I must conduct a search. Will you agree to be my witnesses?"

Vasily nodded, still understanding nothing.

"But where is Tend?"

"He went to the movies with Oxana," said Yegorov.

Vasily silently bowed his head and bit his lip.

"You two go ahead, I'll stay here for a while," he said.

Ten minutes later Yegorov and Samoylenko dragged in a large yellow valise.

"All of Calder's notes are here," said Yegorov, his face red from the strain of lifting the heavy valise.

"I shall have to confiscate all this," Samoylenko said severely.

He took out a folder and made a notation with a worried air. A microfilm camera appeared in his hands.

Vasily watched everything as in a dream. The meaning of the words spoken did not seem to reach him.

"Why did he have to do it? Why?" he muttered.

"What do you mean, why?" Yegorov said excitedly, showing him a bundle of photographs. "Here are the crosses from which Calder decoded the writing of the last Martian. You see these endless geometric designs? Calder discovered from them where the last door to Aiya is to be found! Do you see now?"

"Very well, suppose such a door exists and functions somewhere on Mars," argued Vasily, watching Samoylenko photograph the heavy red crystals. Vasily knew them well: he had pried out thousands of them from the ceiling and walls of the Red Cupola.

"No! No! That isn't it at all!" cried Yegorov. "This door may be the boundary of antispace. It may have extraordinary properties. . . ."

"Very well," Vasily interrupted him. "Suppose this is so. But Calder Disney did not find this door, he merely knew about it. The door remains on Mars, it must still be found. Then why did Angelo have to kill him?"

"Ah, what a fool I am!" Yegorov said quickly. "You don't know the main thing."

He jumped up from his chair.

"Come on, let him work here, he still has a lot to do!" Yegorov pointed at Samoylenko, who was busy photographing the contents of the yellow valise.

Vasily reluctantly followed his friend to the balcony. Yegorov brought him over to the couch, at the head of which hung the mirror from Mars. Its golden rim shone with a cold, glimmering light.

"Feel it," whispered Yegorov.

Vasily touched the rim and snatched away his hand.

"Hot?" laughed Yegorov. He seemed to be highly pleased with everything that happened.

"No, not hot, but—"

"It burns? You see?" Yegorov was anxious to share his secret. "But that isn't the main thing," he said. "Look into the mirror, what do you see there?"

"What? Night, the sickle of the moon, the village," Vasily began to enumerate uncertainly.

"Fine. And what is this? This dark, elongated spot. What is it?"

Vasily peered into the mirror.

"A haystack."

"A haystack? Good, very, very good."

Yegorov went out and soon returned with a glass of water. He put it down on the sofa and took a cigarette lighter from his pocket. Click! and the smoking tongue of flame feebly lit up the night air. There was a smell of benzine. Yegorov brought the flame closer to the mirror, where the haystack loomed darkly. Then he took the fire away.

Vasily cried out. He could not take his eyes from the

127

mirror. The reflection continued to burn there. Yegorov carefully took Vasily by the shoulders and turned him to face the village.

Flames were rising on the horizon. Their bright-orange tongues could be seen clearly even at that distance. Over them floated gray puffs of smoke, dissolving in the darkness. Scarlet rivulets spread out on the ground.

"What have you done?"

"Keep calm!" said Yegorov. He took a mouthful of water from the glass and blew it out at the mirror in a thin spray.

Vasily heard a distant roar and hiss, the flame on the horizon flared once, twice, and went out. Smoke coiled over the stack in the moonlight.

"I daren't pour any more water, or there will be a flood," Yegorov said peacefully.

"So this is it?" Vasily asked softly, pointing at the mirror.

"Yes, brother, that's it," Yegorov began to hurry. "The only unlocked door to Aiya. It was not working on Mars, but here in Musikovka, as you see, it opened up. Rogozhin's Martian had had no time to lock it. And so it stood ajar five million years. Or perhaps it wasn't millions? Angelo decided to use it for his own shady purposes. Now do you understand why he came to you after the Disneys? You saw how it burned? And do you know that your auto-plane, a thousand horsepower strong, was thrown down by a touch of Oxana's little finger? Accidentally, of course. Now do you understand the power of it?"

Vasily understood everything. A medley of disparate events locked themselves into a logical chain.

"What a find!" he whispered, slapping Yegorov on the shoulder. "So we've caught the Martian devil by the tail!"

"We'd better hurry up and make the sign of the cross over him, the foul fiend!" cried Yegorov.

The friends returned to the study.

"Do you have much left to do?" Yegorov asked Samoylenko.

"I am finishing now."

Vasily sat down gloomily.

"What is it?" shouted Yegorov. "You ought to be happy! Such a discovery!"

"I don't know. I cannot imagine an astronaut doing such things. It isn't the first year that Tend has been tramping on planets."

"Finished," Samoylenko sighed with relief and sat down in an armchair, turning his camera on Yegorov and Vasily. "The last of the material evidence. For myself, as a memento."

"Don't, don't!" they waved at him. "What for?"

The door opened and Tend entered the room. He glanced at the sitting men, the open valise, the straps with their shiny buckles, resembling dry snakeskins, the crystals, the photographs, the notes, and understood everything.

Vasily gave him a long pained look. Yegorov and Samoylenko exchanged glances. The latter took a small red notebook and put it on his knee with a bored air. But for some reason he did not get up.

Tend did not give anyone a second glance. He walked out to the balcony. The men in the study quickly looked at each other. They seemed amused at what was about to follow. Angelo returned with the mirror from Mars. He set it down on the floor, tilting it slightly. Then he took the black rod and passed it around the mirror's golden frame. There was a distant ringing hum, as if a jet plane were flying somewhere overhead at a great height. Tend took the bundle of photographs and flung them at the mirror. They disappeared. The crystals from the Red Cupola, the notes, the rolls of tape, the Disney brothers' diary, and the valise with its snakelike straps followed. All the objects vanished without a sound.

But why don't we get up? Yegorov thought with fright.

Tend approached the mirror and looked back.

Yegorov felt that consciousness was slipping from him. A terrible weight pressed down on his head and bent it to his chest. It will burst in a moment, the terrified thought flashed through his mind.

Samoylenko fought the longest. At the very last moment, when Tend began to dissolve in the air, losing his normal shape, the captain tried to jump up. Tend turned his head and the captain fell back into the chair. His camera clicked faintly.

"I did not kill the Disneys. They. . ." Angelo's voice reached the highest notes and broke off.

Samoylenko was justly proud of himself. He had taken the only existing photograph of a live Martian. Three eyes, set at the corners of a perfect triangle, looked out from it with passionate, unearthly power. They were deep and infinitely wise.

Yegorov picked up the gray, glistening oval. The mirror coldly reflected surrounding reality. The last door to Aiya was closed.

And yet, for how long?

7

Homer's Secret

By A. POLESHCHUK

I still do not understand quite how it happened. I have never been so troubled and confused. The whole thing began at the last session of the Moscow Society of Lovers of Ancient Literature. This time there was a stranger in the audience, a man I did not know. He introduced himself to me after the meeting and asked me to visit his school. "I am worried about my boys," he said. "Technology, mathematics, physics—that's all they are interested in. I would like to bring a breath of fresh air into their education." I agreed to come, and was not at all sorry I did.

The graduating class, boys of sixteen and seventeen, listened to me guardedly, and one of them asked after class:

"Have you been sent here to treat our 'technological disease'?"

"No," I replied. "But didn't you find the things I spoke about interesting?"

"Endurable," said one of the boys sitting on the window sill. "Endurable for the time being."

But I knew very well that they were still young, and when the pleasant classroom resounded with the hexameters of ancient tales, the eyes of those self-confident adolescents lit up with admiration and curiosity. In fact, in my classes with students of philology and history I had never encountered such interest and close attention. Evidently, what was merely a required subject to the others was a beguiling web of magical tales to these boys.

I came to them once a week and each time I was struck anew by the freshness of their response and their excellent memory. Only one of them, the tallest and probably the strongest of the youths, asked no questions. He sat in the second row, and his muscular arm, thrown over the back of his chair, swayed rhythmically, marking off the beat of the verse. I addressed him myself from time to time, but his replies were monosyllabic and laconic.

"You speak like a Spartan," I told him once.

This may have been my first mistake.

A month or two went by. I knew that the boys were intensely involved in their studies, completing the assembly of a highly complex apparatus—something like a "time machine"—and that my class was little more than a pedagogical appendage. I was therefore doubly astounded when the silent boy suddenly stopped swinging his arm during my reading and said:

"The stress. It's incorrect. You—"

"Wait, wait," I said. "The stress on this word did not change until the Roman period. Have you begun to study ancient Greek?"

"He's learned it already," broke in one of the boys.

"Is that true?" I asked.

"Oh, no. I simply went through the textbook you told us about. That's all."

"Don't listen to him!" other boys chimed in. "Artem knows the *Iliad* by heart."

"Is that true, Artem?"

"Oh, well, I guess it is."

I asked him a number of questions. Choosing his words without difficulty, Artem replied in the language of Homer. His pronunciation was not always correct but this could easily be remedied.

About ten days ago a dispute broke out between Artem and me. We had just finished reading the passage that relates how Achilles, who had mortally wounded Penthesilea, queen of the Amazons, took her helmet as his legitimate prize and suddenly, struck by her beauty, fell in love with the dying woman.

"There is a theory that the Milesian, Arctinus, the author of this poem, was a pupil of Homer," I remarked.

"I don't doubt it," said Artem. "What a scene!"

"Terrific!" agreed one of the boys.

"Wait, my friends," I said to the whole class. "Can't we find a more suitable expression than 'terrific'?"

"Emotions don't always dictate a careful choice of words. You know this better than anyone else," Artem protested.

"But works like the *Ethiopid* or the *Iliad*—"

"In prettified translations—sure. But Homer's heroes are living people. Sometimes tender, but more often harsh. They wouldn't stop to look for delicate expressions. Achilles cries to Agamemnon, 'Drunk, dogface!' But the translator shilly-shallies and invents ridiculous words: 'Wine bibber, dog-visaged man.' And how does Zeus speak to Hera?" Artem laughed shortly. "That is why Homer is great," he went on. "Always the artist, always the poet. Another would have started the tale of the Trojan war with Adam, but Homer starts with the most important, most vivid thing, "Sing, goddess, the wrath of Achilles, Peleus' son, the ruinous wrath that brought the Achaeans woes without number . . .' "

"You may be right," I began cautiously, leading up to the topic of the day, the question of Homer's identity, "but the whole point is that Homer never existed. . . ."

"What do you mean, 'never existed'? How can that be?" the boys cried.

"Yes, indeed, Homer never existed. There was a collective poet: hundreds of taletellers developed the original nucleus of the legend into a poem of marvelous beauty."

"And this is definitely known?" asked Artem.

"Yes, quite definitely. At least, I personally hold with this view. In the seventeenth century, the Abbe d'Aubignac expressed doubts concerning Homer's identity. Since then, the studies of Grote, Hermann, and, still earlier, Wolf, are considered to have proved it. However, the debate goes further back. At one time, the view of Aristarchus prevailed; he held that Homer created the *Iliad* in his youth, and the *Odyssey* considerably later, when he was already an old man."

"And the ancients? Didn't they think that Homer really existed?" Artem persisted.

"The ancients were unfamiliar with the analytic method, which was developed in the middle of the nineteenth century."

"In such questions, they ought to integrate . . ." someone remarked.

"What did you say? Integrate?" I laughed. "Again your technical terms in a humanities class?"

"Don't be angry," Artem said in a conciliatory voice. "But it is difficult for me and my friends to believe that Homer never lived at all. We must look into it."

"Do you know, boys," I said, "how the ancients dealt with this question? Seven cities fought for the honor of being called the poet's homeland, and there is an ancient verse that came down to us:

*Do not seek to discover where Homer was born and
   lived.*
Proudly all cities think of themselves as his home.
*Do not search for the place, but the spirit; the home of
   the poet*
Is the light of the Iliad *itself, and Odysseus' tale.*

"But that was not all. Homer was regarded as the son of Apollo and the muse Calliope; he was considered to have been a native of Chios, Lydia, Cyprus, Thessaly, Lucca, Rhodes,

134

and Rome. He was even considered to have been a descendant of Odysseus himself, the son of Telemachus and Polycasta, the daughter of Hector."

"Warm!" Artem cried out suddenly. "You're getting warm! It's that last theory that should be looked into. It isn't by chance that Odysseus is so important both in the *Iliad* and the *Odyssey*. There must have been good reasons why the ancient singer . . ."

"Or the ancient singers," I hastened to add.

"No, the ancient singer, chose Odysseus as the central figure of the second poem. Besides, the only song in the *Iliad* which is not directly connected with the theme—the wrath of Achilles and its consequences—is again about the adventures of Odysseus."

"You mean the 'Dolonia'?" I asked.

"I mean the song where Odysseus goes scouting with Diomede and kills the Trojan scout."

"They kill the scout Dolon, and the song is called by specialists the 'Dolonia.' But what follows from this?"

"There was some link between Homer and Odysseus. That's what follows."

"Of course, the archaeologist Schliemann, who made excavations on the site of ancient Troy with the permission of the Turkish Government, never doubted the existence of Odysseus. On the island of Ithaca, where Odysseus was king, Schliemann found the remnants of a stump of an old olive tree amid stone ruins. You remember how Penelope, testing her husband Odysseus, ordered her servant Eurycleia to bring his bed outside, and the offended Odysseus replied:

A secret resides in that bed. I was the one who had built it.
An olive tree, long-leaved and spreading
Grew in our courtyard, its trunk tall as a column.
I erected a stone wall around it, building

135

A bedroom, finished and topped with a roof overhead.
Then I made a strong door, neatly fitted.
After that I cut down the great olive,
Trimmed the trunk, made it round with copper,
Smooth and true, keeping it straight to the line:
Then made I a base for the bed,
Drilling it through with my drill.

"And this was the bed that Schliemann found?" cried Artem.

"Schliemann found the remnants of a giant olive surrounded by stone walls, but this could have been a coincidence. What conclusions can be drawn from that?"

"Many conclusions. After all, this bed was the secret of Odysseus' family, and only he or his son could have known about it. Even the servant Eurycleia did not know that the bed could not be budged! And if Odysseus had really existed, why deny the possibility that Homer did? All this must be checked."

Yes, that was how he put it, "it must be checked." And there was something extraordinary in Artem's words. I recalled to myself the exclamation of one of the boys, "Terrific!" But I said:

"It is not part of my task to 'lure' you away into the ranks of the humanists. I only intended to awaken your interest in the art and history of the ancients. After all, acquaintance with the arts ennobles a man."

"And work over the solution of problems important to mankind does not ennoble men?" asked Artem, getting up.

He walked out of the classroom with rapid strides, and someone remarked:

"Artem always heads straight for the laboratory."

I did not see him again until the memorable day when he approached me and said with a trace of embarrassment:

136

"I have everything ready, we can start out on the search right now."

"The search? For what? For whom?"

"What do you mean, for whom? Homer."

I laughed.

"Homer must be 'sought' in ancient manuscripts, by analyzing and comparing texts, by immersing yourself in a mass of commentaries . . ."

"Or by immersing yourself in the abyss of time," said Artem. "The machine is ready. I thought you would agree."

I was so astounded that I allowed myself to be led to the laboratory. Near the window stood an apparatus gleaming with polished metal, but generally resembling one of those primitive twentieth-century carriages that were powered by storage batteries. I sat down in the metal seat. Artem climbed in beside me. I can truthfully say that I expected nothing serious. I assumed that Artem had simply decided to play a practical joke on me, and that he would burst out laughing and confess. But nothing of the kind took place. He bent down to the control panel, and suddenly the walls of the laboratory slowly began to fade before my eyes. There appeared vague outlines of human figures, who removed the walls with strange movements. The sun flashed for a moment but went out at once. . . .

It took me some time to recover my senses. Our "carriage" rolled down a rocky road. We were surrounded by green woods, and the sun was high overhead. Artem halted the "carriage" at a turn in the road, which opened on a wide view of the sea.

"Where are we?" I asked.

"We'll find out in a moment," Artem replied.

He jumped out of the "carriage" and rapidly began to climb a hill. At the top of the hill sat a man in a yellow garment of unusual cut, but when he rose and bowed to Artem, I noticed that the sleeves had been cut off. Why, it is a chiton! I thought. Immediately beyond the hill the slopes rose steeply, and rocky cliffs loomed high above. And again it was as though a voice whispered in my mind, "Olympus. . . . This is Olympus."

Artem ran skipping down the hill. Hurriedly, he resumed his seat.

"What did you find out?"

"Everything's in order. The goatherd said that Homer was already dead, but the goatherd's grandfather remembered him well."

"What century are we in?" I asked, still disbelieving that all this was happening to me in actuality, not in a dream.

"Now?" Artem bent over the instruments before him and, turned a knob over something resembling a speedometer. "We are in the twelfth century. Before our era, of course. . . ."

There were a few more stops, and then the last. We halted in the middle of a wide meadow. Dusk was falling. A song came wafting to us from a nearby village. We could see the low huts from behind the trees. There was no one around. Artem asked me to get up for a moment, took a package from under the seat, unwrapped it, and offered me a cheese sandwich.

"Where are we now?"

"I am afraid that this time the flight . . ."

Artem bit into his sandwich with appetite, and suddenly, nudging me in the side, pointed in the direction of the village. A horseman galloped out of there across the dewy grass. He approached rapidly, and the clanging of his armor drowned out the barking of the dogs, the song, and the ceaseless chattering of the grasshoppers. The horseman came up to us and halted in astonishment, raising his heavy spear with his right hand. I drew my head into my shoulders, expecting an immi-

138

nent blow, but Artem, without getting up from his seat, raised his hand with the rolled newspaper in which he had wrapped the sandwiches, and loudly greeted the rider in Aeolian.

"Rejoice!" said Artem. "Rejoice!"

"Rejoice too, young warrior, and thou, venerable man," replied the horseman, dismounting.

"We are looking for Homer," said Artem. "Have you seen him?"

"Homer?" the warrior echoed. "Homer . . . No, I know no basileus by that name. Or is it a swineherd who escaped from your household?"

"No, he composes songs."

"Songs? You mean the wandering singer! He was here yesterday and sang for a long time in the square, but may the gods' curse fall upon my head if any of us gave him as much as a dry bone. In other places he fares better; there he still finds stupid dogs who have forgotten what Troy has cost us. The beggar left, he took the road to the sea."

Artem turned a lever and our "carriage" rolled softly across the grass. The horse shied away, startled, and galloped off toward the village, and for a long time afterward we heard the rider's voice, calling him back.

In the morning we saw the sea. The air was transparent, the lineaments of a rocky island seemed to waver in the glittering distance. Artem alighted from the "carriage" and helped me out. The sun was rising in a cloudless blue sky, promising a hot day.

"Someone is sitting there," Artem said, nodding in the direction of the rocky shore.

And indeed, about a hundred yards from us a man sat on a stone. At a distance, he seemed to merge into the gray rocks, but as we came nearer, I saw an old man sitting motionless and staring fixedly at the narrow strip of the far-off island.

We walked toward him.

"It's Homer," said Artem. "It's Homer! This is as true as that island out there is Ithaca."

The old man did not turn at the sound of our steps. He seemed asleep, but when Artem addressed him, he replied to the greeting at once. Yes, the legend was true: Homer was blind.

"He does not see," said Artem. "He is blind."

I looked closely into the old man's face, expecting to see the sightless eyes of the poet, so familiar to us all from the antique bust. But suddenly I realized something else. He was not simply blind. His wrinkled eyelids were deeply sunk into the sockets. Homer had been blinded.

"Homer," I said. "You are speaking to men of the future. Do you understand? Thirty-three centuries divide us."

"Are you gods?" the old man asked simply and loudly.

"No, no! We are mortals, but we have come here from the distant future. You are remembered, Homer, and revered as a great poet. Your songs were written down. Both the *Iliad* and the *Odyssey* . . ."

"Written down? I do not understand."

"Oh, with signs and symbols, on thin white sheets."

"The Phoenicians do this," Homer said thoughtfully. "I have heard of it."

"But I must grieve you. Some people doubt that you really existed, Homer."

"The gods know of no doubts. You are indeed mortals." Homer smiled and felt the rock on which he sat with a quick movement of his strong, nimble hand. Then he bent down and, raising a stone from the ground, held it fast in his hand.

"You see, we are very interested in certain contradictions in your poems."

"You are not mocking me, strangers?" Homer asked

140

loudly, and we could see his still powerful muscles grow tense under his tattered gray cloak.

"Careful!" cried Artem, seizing the old man's hand, raised for a blow.

For a moment Homer resisted, but then his hand relaxed and the stone rolled down the steep slope. And the sea received it with a splash far below.

"Today every man can mock the blind one." Homer spoke sadly. "What do you want of me? Go your way."

"We did not mean to hurt you, we speak the truth. But certain contradictions in your poems. . . . Here, for example, I would like to know. . . . In your songs about Odysseus, you often mention things made of iron, iron weapons. But iron was not yet known in your time."

"Not known? It was not known to those who owned no steep-horned oxen to barter for an axe of hoary iron, a sword or a knife. Have you not met the merchants who bring ornaments and arms from across the sea? They get many captives, and wine, and oxen, and skins for iron."

"Possibly, possibly. But still, you must agree, Homer—"

"Wait," Artem broke in. "It is my turn to ask. Homer, have you eaten today?"

"Neither today, nor yesterday," Homer replied. "Hereabouts, they do not want to hear my songs. Twelve red-cheeked ships, full of valiant warriors, Odysseus, son of Laertes, had taken with him to the steep walls of Ilion, and none have returned. They have not forgotten it here."

Artem ran to our "carriage," took the bundle, and came back, while I used the occasion to ask Homer directly:

"It is thought, Homer, that you were in the ranks of the Achaeans yourself during the war with Troy. Is this true?"

"I was," Homer replied pensively. "And with whom among the heroes do they compare me?"

"With no one," I shrugged. "It is thought that you were an ordinary soldier, and later sang of what you had seen."

Artem came running back. Unwrapping the paper, he gently took Homer's hand and put a slice of bread with cheese into it.

"Eat," said Artem. "This is bread and cheese."

Homer slowly bit off a small piece of the sandwich, swallowed it and hid the rest in the folds of his garment, saying:

"The bread is like air, the cheese tastes good. I believe you, strangers, that you are not mocking a poor old man. Ask me, and I will tell you what I know. . . ."

"From your songs, Homer, we know that, after killing Penelope's suitors, Odysseus became the King of Ithaca again. Did he live long?"

"Some day I shall make a song about this," said Homer. "Not now, later. Yes, Odysseus killed the suitors. Moaning and wailing, their kinsmen carried the bodies away from the house. Those who were Ithacans were buried by their own kin. Those from other cities were sent home. The fishermen were bidden to bring the bodies to each man's kin in their fast ships. But then Eupeithes raised the Cephallenians against him."

"We know, we know," I said. "Allow me, Homer, to read you this passage from memory. 'It is an evil deed, my friends, that this man has contrived for Achaeans! . . . Our names will shame our descendants if we do not avenge our innocent sons and our brothers! . . .' "

"Yes, this is what he said, and led a band of Cephallenians to Odysseus' house."

"And was killed?"

"Yes, he was killed."

"And then, what came then?" Artem asked impatiently.

"The fishermen came to the families of the slain and at night seven black-cheeked ships silently came into Ithaca's harbor. It was late when Odysseus sighted their masts. The

Cephallenians watched how Odysseus fought by his door, some with secret ill will, and some with indifference. The first to be killed was Telemachus, son of Odysseus. Eumaeus was struck by an arrow and died, the swineherd, the loyal, courageous old man. The sword was then stricken from Odysseus' hand, and with leather thongs they bound his hands and his feet. And shouts were raised, 'Kill Odysseus! Death to him, death!' But those who remembered the strength and the wit of the hero, of him who had worn by right the helmet and arms of Achilles, said 'No!' And some stranger called out from the crowd, his eyes burning with hatred, perhaps a kinsman of one who had died at Odysseus' hand, 'Blind him, then.' And they blinded the hero. With laughter they threw him into a boat, and the sea boiled with storm. 'There's a sacrifice to thee, Poseidon, accept it!' they shouted after the boat with the hero. Long was it tossed on the waves, and the sea wind whispered into the sufferer's ears, 'Do you remember how you blinded Polyphemus? We are avenged; live if you can now, hero . . .' "

"And then?"

"The waves cast the boat out onto the sand. Sea gulls were screaming around, fearlessly circling over Odysseus' head. And they screamed, wailing, 'Odysseus, you are alive!' For a long time the hero went wandering, but everyone drove him away. Here some bread, there a cluster of grapes—this was his food. Years passed by. No one dared to acknowledge the hero in the blinded old man. And one evening in Athens Odysseus sat by the fire in the house of a noble, and the master ordered a bowl of broth for the wanderer. Someone sang, the harp strings were ringing. Then the talk turned to the war and the losses, and somebody spoke of Odysseus, saying, 'Troy would not have fallen if cunning Odysseus had not carried his ruse into action so boldly.' So they spoke, and the beggar moved closer to the fire in the hearth. Blind eyes cannot see, but the warmth reached out to him. And the heroes, his friends, suddenly rose all around him. 'You alone have survived us, Odysseus. Can it be that we're lost altogether, gone forever without a trace?' So the heroes addressed him, and Odysseus, remembering all, rose and carefully picking his way with bare feet, walked to the corner where the zither was ringing and timidly asked for it. And taking the strings with his palm, he released them at once. The sound had not died when Odysseus started his song, about Achilles, about his terrible wrath which had brought so much grief to Achaeans. And now the hero walks singing across the length and the breadth of the land that he loves. Some feed him, others turn their hounds upon him, but the fame of the feats of the heroes lives on, and they live in their fame. And often some unknown power drives him back to this shore. He knows—in the mist far away is the shore of his homeland—"

We returned to our apparatus. The "carriage" responded to the touch of Artem's hand. He selected some figures on the control panel. Deep in thought, I lowered myself into the seat.

"The old man considers Odysseus and Homer to be the same person," I said. "I don't know what my colleagues will think of this. Some will unquestionably meet my information without enthusiasm."

"Look, now," said Artem. He was standing on the ground and bent toward me, resting his chest against the side of our "carriage." "Turn this lever toward you."

I obeyed his instruction, and it was only when Artem started back along the path toward the old man, who rose and came to meet him, and their images began to quiver and melt away, that I realized Artem was staying. And from somewhere, strangely distorted, came the old man's cry:

"O Zeus, great father of us all! The gods still live on bright Olympus! Is this you, in truth, my son Telemachus?"

To this day I cannot make sense of all that has happened. Who could have expected it? And least of all, of a man so much in love with technology. Least of all. . . .

8

The White Cone of the Alaid

By A. STRUGATSKY *and* B. STRUGATSKY

Embryomechanics is the science concerned with simulating the processes of biological development and the construction of self-perpetuating mechanisms.

(AUTHOR'S NOTE)

Vakhlakov said to Ashmarin:

"You will go to Shumshu Island."

"Where is that?" Ashmarin asked glumly.

"Northern Kuriles. You're flying today, at twenty-thirty. Passenger-freight plane, 'Novosibirsk-Port Providenya.' "

The mechano-embryos were to be tested under various conditions. The Institute dealt chiefly with interplanetary matters. Hence, thirty of its forty-seven groups were assigned to other planets and the moon. The other seventeen worked on earth.

"Very well," Ashmarin said slowly.

He had hoped for an interplanetary assignment, or at least a lunar one, and he had every reason to expect it. He had been feeling fine lately—better, in fact, than for a long time. He was in excellent shape and he clung to his hope until the very last moment. But for some reason Vakhlakov decided otherwise, and one could not even have a proper talk with him: two blank-faced strangers sat in the office, and Ashmarin would not speak in their presence.

"Very well," he repeated calmly.

"North Kurilsk is already informed of your coming," said Vakhlakov. "You will decide on the test site in Baikovo."

"Where is that?"

"On Shumshu. It is the administrative center of the island." Vakhlakov linked his hands and stared at the wall. "Sermus is also staying on Earth," he said. "He will go to the Sahara."

Ashmarin said nothing.

"Well," said Vakhlakov. "I have chosen your assistants. You will have two assistants. Good men."

"Beginners," said Ashmarin.

"They will do well," Vakhlakov said quickly. "They've had general training. They are good men, I tell you. They know what to do in any situation."

The strangers in the office smiled respectfully. Vakhlakov added:

"Incidentally, one of them was also with the 'Astronaut Explorers.' "

"Fine," said Ashmarin. "Is that all?"

"That's it. Good luck. Your load and your men are in one-sixteen."

Ashmarin went to the door. Vakhlakov waited a moment then called after him:

"And come back soon, *Kamerad*. I have an interesting theme for you."

Ashmarin closed the door behind him and stood for a while. Then he remembered that Laboratory 116 was five floors lower and walked to the elevator. In the elevator he met Tatsudzo Misima, a thickset Japanese with a shaven head and blue eyeglasses. Misima asked:

"Where is your group going, Fyodor Semyonovich?"

"The Kuriles," Ashmarin answered.

Misima blinked his swollen eyelids, took out his handkerchief, and began to polish his glasses. Ashmarin knew that Misima's group was assigned to Mercury, to the Burning Plateau. Misima was twenty-eight years old and he had not yet flown his first billion kilometers. The elevator stopped.

"Sayonara, Tatsudzo. Good luck," said Ashmarin.

Misima smiled broadly.

"Sayonara, Fyodor-san," he answered.

Laboratory 116 was bright and shiny. In the corner on the right stood The Egg—a polished sphere half the height of a man. In the left corner sat two men. When Ashmarin came in, they rose. Ashmarin stopped, examining them. One was tall, fair-haired, with a homely red face. The other, shorter, was a dark, handsome young man of Spanish type, in a suede jacket and heavy mountain-climbing boots. Ashmarin put his hands in his pockets, rose on his toes, and lowered himself back on his heels. Beginners, he thought. He felt a sudden dull ache in his right side, where two ribs were missing.

"Good morning," he said. "My name is Ashmarin."

The dark young man showed his white teeth.

"We know, Fyodor Semyonovich." He stopped smiling and introduced himself: "Kuzma Vladimirovich Sorochinsky."

"Galtsev, Victor Sergeyevich," said the fair-haired one.

I wonder which of them was with the Astronauts, thought Ashmarin. The Spaniard, most likely—Kuzma Sorochinsky. He asked:

"Which of you was with the Astronauts?"

"I was," said fair-haired Galtsev.

"And why were you . . .?" asked Ashmarin. "If it is not a secret . . ."

"No secret," answered Galtsev. "Discipline."

He looked directly into Ashmarin's eyes. Galtsev had light-blue eyes and fluffy eyelashes, like a girl's. They somehow did not match his rough-hewn face.

"Yes," said Ashmarin. "An Astronaut must be disciplined. Every man must be disciplined. However, this is only my opinion. What can you do?"

He saw Galtsev's brows knit and asked again, with something like satisfaction:

"What can you do, Galtsev?"

"I am a biologist," said Galtsev. "My field of specialization is nematodes."

"Ah . . ." said Ashmarin, and turned to Sorochinsky. "And you?"

"Engineer-gastronomist," said Sorochinsky, displaying his white teeth again.

Delightful, thought Ashmarin. A specialist in gut-worms and a pastry cook. An undisciplined Astronaut and a suede jacket. Fine fellows. Especially this wretched Astronaut. The devil take that Vakhlakov. Ashmarin visualized Vakhlakov carefully and scrupulously selecting his interplanetary personnel out of two thousand volunteers, then glancing at his watch, glancing at the lists, and saying: "Ashmarin's group. The Kuriles. Ashmarin is a good, experienced man. He'll manage with three assistants. Even two. After all, this is not Mercury, not the Burning Plateau. He can have this Sorochinsky, and . . . oh, Galtsev. Especially since Galtsev has also been with the Astronauts."

"Are you prepared for this job?" asked Ashmarin.

"Yes," said Galtsev.

"Quite prepared, Fyodor Semyonovich!" said Sorochinsky. "Thoroughly trained."

Ashmarin went up to The Egg and touched its cool, polished surface. Then he asked:

"Do you know what this is? You, Galtsev?"

Galtsev raised his eyes to the ceiling, thought a moment, and said in a monotone:

"Embryo-mechanical device MZ-8. Mechano-embryo, Model 8. Autonomous, self-developing, mechanical system incorporating the VMC program—Vakhlakov's Mechano-Chromosome—a system of receptors and performing organs, a digesting system, and an energy system. The MZ-8 is an embryo-mechanical device capable of developing into any programmed construction under any conditions and using any raw materials. The MZ-8 is intended to . . ."

"You," said Ashmarin to Sorochinsky. Sorochinsky answered without hesitation:

"The given sample of the MZ-8 is intended to be tested under terrestrial conditions. The program is standard. Standard 64: development of the embryo into a hermetic cupola to house six persons, with a vestibule and an oxygen filter."

Ashmarin looked out of the window and asked:

"Weight?"

"Approximately 150 pounds."

"Good," said Ashmarin. "And now I will tell you what you do not know. First, The Egg cost nineteen thousand man-hours of skilled labor. Second, it weights exactly 150 pounds, and, whenever necessary, you will carry it."

Galtsev nodded. Sorochinsky said:

"We will, Fyodor Semyonovich."

"Excellent," said Ashmarin. "You may begin right now. Roll it over to the elevator and take it down into the lobby. Then go to the warehouse and get the registering apparatus. Report with the entire load at the city airport by 8 P.M. Don't be late."

He turned and walked out. Behind him there was a heavy, rumbling sound: Ashmarin's group had begun to carry out its first assignment.

At dawn, the stratospheric passenger-freight plane dropped the group by pterocar over the Second Kuriles Strait. Galtsev brought the pterocar out of its dive, glanced around, looked at the map, at the compass, and immediately located Baikovo. It consisted of several rows of two-story buildings of white and red lithoplastic, arranged in a semicircle around a small, deep

bay. The pterocar landed on the embankment. An early pas-
ser-by, a young man in a jersey shirt and ducks, directed
them to the administration building. The acting administrator
of the island, an elderly, stooped Ainu who was also the senior
agronomist, welcomed them pleasantly.

When Ashmarin explained his assignment, the administrator suggested a choice of several low hills along the north
shore. He spoke Russian quite well, but occasionally halted in
the middle of a word, as though uncertain of the stress, or perhaps stuttering slightly.

"The north shore is quite far," he said. "And there are no
decent roads to it. But you have a pterocar. And then, I
cannot offer you anything nearer. I don't know much about
experiments in physics. But most of the island is occupied by
melon fields and greenhouses. Students are working everywhere now. I cannot take r-risks."

"There is no risk of any kind," said Sorochinsky. "None
whatever."

Ashmarin remembered how he had spent a whole hour,
two years earlier, on a fire escape, trying to get away from a
plastic vampire which needed protoplasm for its own processes. True, there had been no Egg as yet at that time.

"Thank you," he said. "The north shore will be fine."

"Yes," said the Ainu. "There are no melon fields and no
greenhouses there, only birch thicket. And also, a party of
arche-ologists is working somewhere in the area."

"Archeologists?" Sorochinsky wondered.

"Thank you," said Ashmarin. "I think we shall start right
now."

"Have breakfast first," said the Ainu.

They ate silently.

"Thanks," said Ashmarin, getting up. "We'll have to
hurry."

"Good-bye," said the Ainu. "If you need anything, don't hesit-ate to ask."

"No, we will not hesit-ate," said Sorochinsky.

Ashmarin glanced at him quickly and turned back to their host.

"Good-bye," he said.

In the pterocar, Ashmarin said:

"If you allow yourself another antic of this kind, I shall kick you off the island."

"Sorry," said Sorochinsky, blushing. The blush made his dark, smooth face still more handsome.

On the north shore there were, indeed, no melon fields or greenhouses; there was nothing but birch. The Kuriles birch grows lying down, it spreads over the ground, and its damp, gnarled stems and branches form thick, impassable tangles. From the air, the thickets of the Kuriles birch look like innocent green lawns, quite suitable for landing small craft. Neither Galtsev, who piloted the pterocar, nor Ashmarin or Sorochinsky had any idea of what the Kuriles birch was like. Ashmarin pointed to a round knoll and said, "Here." Sorochinsky timidly glanced at Ashmarin and said, "A good spot." Galtsev dropped the landing gear and brought the pterocar down directly in the middle of a wide green field at the foot of the round hill. Its nose buried itself with a crashing noise in the stunted greenery of the Kuriles birch. Ashmarin heard the crash, saw millions of varicolored stars, and blacked out.

The first thing he saw when he opened his eyes again was a hand. It was large and sunburned, and its freshly bruised fingers moved slowly, as though reluctantly, over the instrument board. The hand disappeared, and a dark-red face appeared, its blue eyes rimmed with feminine eyelashes.

"Comrade Ashmarin," said Galtsev, moving his cut lips with difficulty.

151

Ashmarin groaned and tried to sit up. His right side hurt badly, and his forehead seemed to smart. He touched his forehead and brought his fingers to his eyes. The fingers were bloody. He looked at Galtsev, who was wiping his mouth with his handkerchief.

"An expert landing," said Ashmarin. "You delight me, comrade specialist in nematodes."

Galtsev was silent. He pressed his crushed handkerchief to his lips, and his face was immobile. Sorochinsky's voice, high and quivering, said:

"It isn't his fault, Fyodor Semyonovich."

Ashmarin turned his head and looked at Sorochinsky. The young man's hair was rumpled.

"It is not Galtsev's fault," he repeated and moved away.

Ashmarin opened the door of the cabin a little, put out his head and stared for a few moments at the uprooted, broken stems entangled in the landing gear. He stretched his hand, tore off a few stiff, shiny leaves, rubbed them in his fingers and tried them on his teeth. The leaves were acrid and bitter. Ashmarin spat and asked without looking at Galtsev:

"Is the craft intact?"

"It is intact," answered Galtsev through his handkerchief.

"You knocked out a tooth?" asked Ashmarin.

"Yes," said Galtsev.

"It'll heal before your wedding day," promised Ashmarin. "Try to get the craft to the hilltop."

It was not easy to break out of the idiotic thicket, but in the end Galtsev brought the pterocar to the top of the round hill. Ashmarin, stroking his right side with his hand, climbed out and looked around. From here the island seemed deserted and as flat as a table. The hill was bare and reddish from volcanic slag. In the east, dense thickets of Kuriles birch were climbing up its slope. In the south, the green rectangles of melon fields spread out into the distance. The south shore was some seven kilometers away. Beyond it were pale-lilac mountaintops in a haze of violet mist. And still farther to the right a strange triangular cloud with sharp outlines hung motionless in the blue sky. The north shore was much nearer. It dropped abruptly into the sea, and over the sheer drop a tower jutted out absurdly—the top, most likely, of an ancient Japanese fort. Near the tower a tent gleamed white, and tiny figures moved about. They were the archeologists mentioned by the acting administrator. Ashmarin sniffed. The air smelled of salt water and sun-heated stone. And it was very quiet; even the sea could not be heard.

A good spot, thought Ashmarin. The Egg could be left right there with the movie cameras and the rest of the equipment on the slopes. And the camp could be set up below in a melon field. The melons were probably still green. Then he thought about the archeologists. They must be at least five kilometers away, but they ought to be warned in any case, so that they would not be alarmed when the embryo began to develop. What could archeologists be doing here? Ashmarin called Galtsev and Sorochinsky and said:

"The experiment will take place here. I think the site is suitable. The raw material—lava, tufa—is just what is needed. You can start now."

Galtsev and Sorochinsky went to the pterocar and opened the baggage compartment. A spray of sun-flecks burst out of it—reflections from The Egg. Sorochinsky climbed in, grunted, and pushed The Egg out onto the ground with a single heave. Crunching on the gravel, The Egg rolled a few feet and came to a halt. Galtsev barely had time to jump aside.

"Ridiculous," he said quietly. "You'll rupture yourself."

Sorochinsky jumped down and said in a deep basso:

"It's all right, we're accustomed to hard work."

Ashmarin walked around The Egg, tried to push it. The Egg did not even rock.

"Excellent," said Ashmarin. "Now the movie cameras."

They worked for a long time setting up the movie cameras: one with an infrared lens, another with a stereolens, a third with a lens registering temperature characteristics, and a fourth with an assortment of light filters.

It was almost noon when Ashmarin carefully mopped his perspiring forehead with his sleeve and took from his pocket a small plastic container holding the activator. Galtsev and Sorochinsky stood close behind him, looking over his shoulder. Ashmarin unhurriedly shook the activator out onto his palm. It was a shiny tube with a suction piece at one end and a red, indented button at the other.

"Let's start," he said aloud. He approached The Egg and pressed the suction piece to the polished metal. After a moment's pause, he pressed the red button with his thumb.

Now only a direct hit from a rocket gun could halt the processes started under the shiny casing. A series of high-frequency impulses roused the mechanism into action. Hundreds of micro-receptors fed information on the environment to the positron brain and the mechano-chromosome. The mechano-embryo was being set to function under the given field conditions. No one knew how long the process would take. But as soon as it was properly set, the mechanism would begin to develop.

Ashmarin glanced at his watch. It was twelve-zero-five. With a slight effort, he separated the activator from the surface of The Egg, replaced it in the case and slipped it into his pocket. Then he looked at Galtsev and Sorochinsky. They were staring silently at The Egg. Ashmarin touched The Egg for the last time and said:

"Let's go."

Ashmarin ordered Galtsev to stop halfway between the hill and the melon fields. The Egg was in full view from here—a silver sphere on the rusty hill under a blue sky. Sending Sorochinsky to the archeologists, Ashmarin sat down on the grass in the shade of the pterocar. Galtsev was already dozing under the pterocar, where he had stretched to escape the heat of the sun. Ashmarin smoked, glancing up from time to time, now at the summit of the hill, and now at the strange triangular cloud in the west. Finally he took up his field glasses. As he had expected, the triangular cloud solidified into a snowy peak of some mountain, probably a volcano. Through the field glasses, he could see dark, narrow strips of bare land where the snow had melted and some patches of snow below the jagged white edge. Ashmarin put aside the field glasses and thought that The Egg would probably open at night, and that would be good, for daylight affected the work of the cameras. His mind turned to Sermus, who must have had a violent argument with Vakhlakov, but had probably gone to the Sahara in the end anyway. Then it occurred to him that Misima must be loading up now at the rocket-launching pad in Kirghizia, and again he felt the dull ache in his right side. "Old and feeble," he muttered, and glanced sideways at Galtsev. The young man was lying face down, his head on his hands.

An hour and a half later, Sorochinsky returned. He was stripped to the waist, and his dark smooth skin was shiny with perspiration. He carried his suede jacket and his shirt under his arm. Sorochinsky squatted down in front of Ashmarin and, his teeth glinting as he spoke, reported that the archeologists were grateful for the warning and very interested in the experiment. The archeological party consisted of four persons; they were assisted by students from Baikovo and North Kurilsk; they were excavating underground Japanese fortifications dating back to the middle of the last century, and their chief was "a very charming girl."

155

' Ashmarin thanked him and asked him to prepare dinner. He sat in the shadow of the pterocar, chewing at a blade of grass and squinting at the distant white cone. Sorochinsky wakened Galtsev and they went to work nearby, talking in an undertone.

"I'll get the soup," said Sorochinsky, "and you take care of the entree, Vitya."

"We have chicken somewhere," Galtsev said in a voice still hoarse with sleep.

"Here is some chicken," said Sorochinsky. "The archeologists are excellent fellows. They're excavating Japanese entrenchments of the forties of the last century. They had an underground fortress here, with a garrison of twenty thousand men. Then the Soviet armies knocked them out—or, rather, captured them, with all their guns and tanks. One of the archeologists, a bearded fellow, gave me this—a revolver cartridge. Look!"

Galtsev mumbled, annoyed:

"Get this rusty trash away from here."

The fragrance of the boiling soup spread through the air.

"Their chief," continued Sorochinsky, "is quite a girl. Blonde, slender, pretty. She took me to a pillbox and made me look out of the gunport. The entire north shore, she told me, was under fire from there."

"So?" asked Galtsev. "Was it really?"

"Who knows! Probably. But I looked mostly at her. Then we measured the thickness of the ceiling."

"For two hours?"

"U-huh. Then it came to me that she had the same name as the bearded fellow, so I took off. And those dungeons, I must tell you, are damned unpleasant. Dark, with mold on the walls. Where's the bread?"

"Here," said Galtsev. "Maybe she is only his sister?"

"Maybe," said Sorochinsky. "And how's The Egg?"

156

"Nohow," answered Galtsev.

"All right now," said Sorochinsky. "Fyodor Semyonovich, dinner's served!"

During the meal, Sorochinsky declared that the Japanese word *totika* was derived from the Russian *ognevaya tochka*—"firing point," while the Russian world *dot*—"pillbox"—came from the English "dot," which also means "point." Then he began to talk at great length about pillboxes, casemates, embrasures, the density of fire to the square meter, and so on. Ashmarin ate as quickly as he could and refused dessert. After dinner he left Galtsev to watch The Egg, while he climbed into the pterocar and took a nap. It was astonishingly quiet. Only Sorochinsky, who was washing the dishes in the brook, broke the silence by humming from time to time. Galtsev sat with the field glasses and did not take his eyes away from the hilltop for a moment.

When Ashmarin woke, the sun was setting. Dark-violet dusk was gathering from the south. It was becoming cool. The mountains in the west had turned black, and the cone of the volcano hung like a gray shadow over the horizon. The Egg on the hilltop gleamed fiery red. A blue-gray mist drifted over the melon fields. Galtsev was sitting in the same pose, listening to Sorochinsky.

"In Astrakhan," Sorochinsky was saying, "I once ate a 'shah's rose.' It's an extraordinary melon. Beautiful, and tastes like pineapple."

Galtsev cleared his throat.

Ashmarin sat without moving for a few moments longer, aware of the ache in his side. He remembered how he had eaten melons with Gorbovsky on Venus. A whole shipload of melons had been brought to the planetological station from Earth. They ate the melons, biting into the crisp pulp, the juice trickling down their chins. Then they shot the slippery black seeds at one another with their fingers.

157

"Delicious. I can tell you as a gourmet!"

"Hush," said Galtsev. "You'll wake the Old Man."

Ashmarin arranged himself more comfortably, rested his chin on the back of the front seat, and closed his eyes. The cabin was warm and a trifle stuffy. The plastic metal cooled slowly.

"So you never flew with the Old Man?" asked Sorochinsky.

"No," said Galtsev.

"I am a bit sorry for him. Also envious. He has lived a life I'll never see. Nor will many others. And yet, it's over."

"Why over?" asked Galtsev. "He has merely stopped flying."

"A bird that has stopped flying . . ." Sorochinsky fell silent. "Generally, it's the end of all you pioneering Astronauts."

"Nonsense," Galtsev said calmly.

Ashmarin heard Sorochinsky turn where he sat.

"There," he said. "There it is now. They will be produced in the hundreds and dropped over unknown and dangerous worlds. And every Egg will build a city, a rocket-landing field, a space ship. The Eggs will dig and work mines and quarries. They will hunt and study your nematodes. And the Astronauts will merely collect the data and skim their various creams."

"Nonsense," repeated Galtsev. "Cities, mines . . . And what about the hermetic bubble for six men?"

"What about the hermetic bubble?"

"Who will those six be?"

"All the same," said Sorochinsky. "All the same, it's the end of the Explorers. The hermetic bubble is only a beginning. Automatic space ships will be sent overhead to drop The Eggs. And men will come only when everything else is ready. . . ."

He began to discuss the future of embryo-mechanics, obviously quoting Vakhlakov's well-known report. They talk a lot about it now, thought Ashmarin. And it's all true. When the first automatic interplanetary ships had been tested, people had also said that men would from then on only skim the cream. And when Akimov and Sermus had launched the first SCYSC—system of cybernetic scouts—Ashmarin had wanted to quit the Explorers. This had been twenty years before, but he had since jumped many times straight into hell after mangled fragments of SCYSC's to do what they had been unable to accomplish. Of course, the automatic ships and SCYSC's and embryo-mechanics enormously enlarged man's power, but mechanisms could never fully replace man's living brain and hot blood. And never would. A beginner, thought Ashmarin of Sorochinsky. And he babbles too much.

When Galtsev said "Nonsense" for the fourth time, Ashmarin climbed out of the car. Sorochinsky fell silent and jumped up. In his hands he held half of an unripe melon, with a knife stuck in it. Galtsev continued sitting as he was, on folded legs.

"Would you like some melon, Fyodor Semyonovich?" asked Sorochinsky.

Ashmarin shook his head and, putting his hands into his pockets, began to look at the hilltop. The red glints on the polished surface of The Egg dimmed rapidly. Night was descending quickly. A vivid star rose suddenly out of the fog and slowly began to climb the dense blue sky.

"Sputnik Eight," said Galtsev.

"No," Sorochinsky said confidently. "It's Sputnik Seventeen. Or no, it's Sputnik Mirror."

Ashmarin, who knew that it was Sputnik Eight, clenched his teeth and walked toward the hill. He was thoroughly tired of Sorochinsky; besides, he had to inspect the cameras.

On his way back, he saw a fire. The restless Sorochinsky had lit a bonfire and was now standing in a picturesque pose, waving his arms.

". . . a goal is only a means," Ashmarin heard. "Happiness is not in happiness itself, but in the race for it . . ."

"I read this somewhere," said Galtsev.

So did I, thought Ashmarin. Should I order Sorochinsky to go to bed? Ashmarin glanced at his watch. The luminous hands pointed to midnight. It was completely dark.

The Egg burst at 2:53 A.M. The night was moonless. Ashmarin dozed, sitting hear the fire, his right side turned toward its warmth. Red-faced Galtsev nodded next to him. On the other side of the fire, Sorochinsky sat reading a newspaper, rustling its pages. And then The Egg burst.

There was a sharp, piercing sound. Then the hilltop glowed with an orange light. Ashmarin glanced at his watch and got up. The summit of the hill stood out clearly against the starry sky. And when their eyes became accustomed to the darkness, they all saw a multitude of faint, reddish sparks, slowly shifting around the spot where The Egg was sitting.

"It has started!" Sorochinsky uttered in an awed whisper. "It has started! Vitya, wake up, it has started!"

"Will you be quiet for once?" Galtsev said quickly. He also spoke in a whisper.

Of all three, only Ashmarin knew what was taking place on the hilltop. The first ten hours after activation, the mechano-embryo was busy tuning itself in to its environment. The general commands fed into the positron-directing mechanism were modified and corrected in accordance with the external temperature, atmospheric composition, atmospheric pressure, humidity, and dozens of other factors reported by the receptors. The digesting system—the magnificent "high-frequency stomach" of the embryo-mechanical system—was being adapted to process lava and tufa into polymerized lithoplastic; the neutron accumulators prepared themselves to release the exact amounts of energy necessary for the various processes. When the tuning up was completed, the mechanism began to develop. Everything in The Egg that was not needed for development under the given conditions was used in the alteration

160

and strengthening of the functioning organs—the effectors. Then came the turn of the casing. The casing was broken, and the mechano-embryo began to utilize the raw materials around it.

The sparks increased in number and moved ever more rapidly. Shrill buzzing and grinding sounds filled the air: the effectors were biting into the rock and reducing the lumps of tufa to dust. Puffs of reddish smoke broke from the hilltop and rose silently into the starry sky. Their quivering, faint glow would illuminate for a moment the heavy, lumbering forms below, then everything would disappear again. The grinding and crashing increased.

"Can we go nearer?" Sorochinsky asked in a pleading voice.

Ashmarin did not answer. He suddenly remembered the test of the first mechano-embryo, the ancestor of The Egg, several years before. At that time he had been a newcomer to embryo-mechanics. The mechano-embryo had been set up in a large pavilion near the Institute. It consisted of eighteen cases resembling fireproof safes, ranged along the walls with a huge pile of cement in the center. Under the pile of cement were hidden the effector and digesting systems. Vakhlakov had motioned with his hand, and someone had turned on the switch. They had sat in the pavilion till late into the night, forgetting everything in the world. The pile of cement was melting, and by evening the outlines of a standard lithoplastic house—with three rooms, steam heat, and an autonomous electrical system—appeared out of the steam and smoke. It was almost exactly like the prefabricated houses produced by factories. The only difference was that a ceramic cube—the "stomach"—and some complex combinations of hemo-mechanical effectors remained in the bathroom. Vakhlakov had inspected the house, touched the effectors with his toe, and said:

161

"I guess we're done with initial experimentation. It's time to build The Egg."

That was the first time the word had been uttered. Afterward came a great deal of work, some successes, and very many failures. Embryo-mechanical systems were "learning" to set themselves, to adapt themselves to sharp changes of environment, to repair and reconstitute themselves. They were "learning" to serve man reliably under the most complex and dangerous conditions. They were "learning" to evolve into houses, excavators, and rockets. They were "learning" not to get smashed when dropped from great heights, not to melt under waves of molten metal, not to fear absolute zero. Hundreds of people, dozens of research institutes and laboratories had helped the mechano-embryo to become what it was now—The Egg. No, it was a good thing, after all, that Ashmarin had had to remain on Earth!

On the hilltop, the puffs of glowing smoke flew up ever more frequently; the crashing, grinding, and buzzing coalesced into a steady flow of jangling noise. The wandering red sparks formed chains, and the chains wove themselves into fantastic, moving lines. A rosy glow was rising over them, and it was already possible to distinguish something huge, humped, rocking like a ship on waves.

Ashmarin looked at his watch again. It was five minutes to four. Evidently, the lava and tufa had proved to be excellent materials. The bubble was growing much faster than with cement. It will be interesting to see, he thought, what the temperature records will show. The mechanism was building the cupola from the top down toward the edges, and the effectors were digging deeper and deeper into the mound. To make sure the bubble would not end up underground, the mechano-embryo would have to provide itself with pile supports, or else to move the bubble away from the pit dug by the effectors. Ashmarin visualized the white-hot edges of the cupola, to which the blades of the effectors were adding more and more of the lithoplastic processed from the ground materials.

For a moment the hilltop was immersed in silence. The crashing stopped, giving way to a faint buzzing. The mechanism was resetting its energy system.

"Sorochinsky," said Ashmarin.

"Yes?" Sorochinsky answered from the darkness.

"Go around the hill on the right, and watch what's happening from there. You're not to go up the hill under any circumstances."

"I'm running, Fyodor Semyonovich."

In a whisper, he asked Galtsev for a flashlight, and then the yellow circle of light began to jump over the gravel and disappeared.

The clattering resumed. A rosy glow relit the hill. It seemed to Ashmarin that the cupola had shifted a little, but he was not sure. He thought with regret that he should have sent Sorochinsky to the other side of the hill earlier, as soon as the embryo had broken out of The Egg. However, in time the cameras would provide all needed information.

Suddenly there was a deafening blast. A flare of red burst over the hilltop. Crimson lightning crept down the black slope. The pink glow became yellow and vivid and disappeared at once behind a curtain of thick smoke. A violent crash split the sky, and Ashmarin looked with horror at the huge shadow rising amid the smoke and flame that enveloped the summit. Something massive and lumbering, sending out glints of light, swayed on thin, wavering legs. Another blast, another molten lightning zigzagging down the slope. The earth shook and the shadow hanging in the smoky glare collapsed.

Ashmarin rushed up the hill. Inside it something was crashing and splitting; waves of fiery air almost knocked him off his feet; and in the dancing red light he saw the movie cameras—the sole witnesses of what had just occurred—

toppling down and carrying pieces of lava along with them. He stumbled over one camera. It was lying on its side, the bent legs of the tripod sprawled out. He slowed down, while hot gravel rolled down the hillside in his path. It was quiet now at the summit, but something was still glowing up there in the smoke. Then there was another thump, and Ashmarin saw a feeble yellow flash.

At the top there was a smell of hot smoke and something unfamiliar and sour. He stopped at the edge of a huge crater. Properly speaking, it was not a crater, but a pit with vertical walls, and lying on its side in it was the almost-finished hermetic bubble for six persons, with a vestibule and an oxygen filter. The pit was lined with glowing slag, and Ashmarin could see against the glow the helpless movement of the hemo-mechanical tentacles which had lost their controls. From the pit came a smell of something burnt and sour.

"But what can it be?" asked Sorochinsky.

Ashmarin sat down on the rim of the pit and cautiously began to descend.

"Don't!" cried Galtsev. "It's dangerous."

"Silence!" snapped Ashmarin.

He had to know at once what had happened. It could not be due to any fault in the construction of The Egg, the most perfect machine created by man. The most invulnerable machine, the most intelligent machine.

A blast of heat scorched his face. Ashmarin closed his eyes and slipped down past the red-hot edge of the cupola. He stood up and looked around. He saw at once the partly melted concrete vaults, the blackened, rusty shafts of the framework, a wide dark passage leading somewhere into the depths of the hill. He took a step forward, but almost fell over something heavy and round. Ashmarin bent down. It took him a moment to recognize the gray metal object with a thick, round tip. When he did, he understood everything. It was an artillery shell.

The hill was hollow. A hundred years ago some scoundrels had built in it a dark, concrete-lined vault and stored their shells there. The embryo had had no way of knowing that there was an ammunition dump beneath it, storing shells. It did not know what an artillery shell was, for the men who had programmed it had long forgotten that there were once such things as shells. As Ashmarin recalled, shells were charged with trotyl. Now one of these shells had exploded—set off by the heat, or the jolt. Everything explosive had begun to blow up. And the remarkable machine was turned into a heap of rubble.

There was a shower of pebbles from above. Ashmarin glanced up and saw Galtsev climbing down to join him. Sorochinsky was coming down the opposite wall.

"Where are you going?" asked Ashmarin.

"We want to help you, Fyodor Semyonovich."

"I don't need you," said Ashmarin.

"We're only . . ." began Sorochinsky and broke off.

A crack ran down the wall behind him. The cupola rocked.

"Careful!" yelled Sorochinsky.

Ashmarin stepped aside, stumbled on the shell, and fell. He fell face down, but turned on his back at once. The cupola was falling straight upon him. He shut his eyes and heard someone's choked growl. It was his own growl when the fiery edge of the cupola hit him.

One could simply lie and look up into the blue sky. He had not looked at the blue sky for such a long time, and it was worth looking at for hours. He had known it as an Explorer when he had parachuted onto the North Pole of Venus, when he had stormed Iapetus, when he had sat alone on his crashed planetoplane on Transpluto. Out there, there had been no sky at all. Nothing but starry vacuum and a dazzling star—the sun. At that time, it seemed to him that he would give the last minutes of his life for a glimpse of blue sky. On Earth this feeling is quickly forgotten. Only when disaster comes do you remember, and each time it seems too late. And then sometimes you find it was not too late.

"Will he live?" asked Sorochinsky's voice.

Ashmarin did not know to whom the words referred—to him or Galtsev. Galtsev lay next to him. He was unconscious and moaned quietly. He had burned himself pulling Ashmarin out from under the cupola. Sorochinsky was also badly burned.

I must live, thought Ashmarin.

An Explorer does not think of death. Besides, the catastrophe, after all, had been caused by such an impossible, such a preposterous chance. How could he have suspected that the mound contained an ancient Japanese fort, that the long, ugly paw of century-old crimes would stretch out to reach him? He remembered the times when every second might have been his last. He had once lain like this before, mangled, face up. Only the sky had been different. The sky had been orange-black; long dark streaks extended across it, a noxious hurricane blew over him; and no one was around. There had been nothing but pain, nausea, and—as now—regret that everything was coming to an end.

He looked intently at the blue sky, and it seemed to him that pale spots appeared and swam away in the blue. He strained to understand what it was, and why. Then he understood: he wanted to see the strange immobile clear-edged cloud. With an effort he raised his head. Someone's hand supported his neck. And he saw the transparent white cone over the horizon.

"What is it?" he asked.

"It is the volcano, Alaid," said someone.

"It would be good to go up there . . ." said Ashmarin.

He lowered his head and began to think that one day he would climb this cone. He would wear heavy mountaineer's boots like Sorochinsky's. He might even take Sorochinsky with him. The air up there must be cold, so cold it would chill your teeth.

"What a good, blue sky," said Ashmarin aloud. He closed his eyes and thought that the pain was receding. And all at once he wanted to sleep.

Ashmarin dozed, and it seemed to him that he was standing on the white summit of the Alaid and looking up into the blue sky. You can look at it for hours—it is so blue, and so beautifully of the Earth. A sky to which men return.

9

Out in Space

LILAC PLANET

"I see no sense in going on with the digging. We have quite enough material to tell what happened here. I give you ten days to pack the exhibits. The freight jet and the "Meteor" will start in twenty days. I hope there are no objections?"

"There are."

The Commander frowned with annoyance.

"The same old doubts?"

"Yes."

"It seems to me that we have discussed the matter sufficiently. After all, there is nothing remarkable in the history of the planet. Long evolution, resulting in the emergence of intelligent beings who achieved a high level of development; sudden invasion of cosmic conquerors; enslavement of the natives of the planet; a period of cultural decline; extinction of the newcomers who failed to adapt completely to unfamiliar conditions of existence; an era of revival and, finally, the inevitable aging of the planet and resettlement in another part of the galaxy. What troubles you in this entirely self-evident chain of events?"

"What troubles me is that none of this is true. The more you try to tie up the facts into a logical whole, the more obviously incongruous they become."

"Well! I am willing to listen to your arguments once more."

For a few moments the Doctor was silent, collecting his thoughts.

"Very well. I'll start from the beginning. First, by the time of the supposed invasion the planet's population was at a very high level of development. They were already able to use nuclear energy, they had an advanced industry, and they spoke a single language. Judging from everything, there were no internal conflicts of any kind on the planet. Do you really think they would have submitted to invaders without a struggle? And yet we did not discover any traces of battles, inevitable in such situations.

"Second, if the invaders were capable of cosmic flights, they should have left on the planet some elements of their specific culture. But the period of enslavement is characterized only by the decline of the native culture. The newcomers, those two-legged rats, seem to have brought with them nothing but a blind thirst for destruction, cannibalism, and eradication of all moral values.

"Third, the period of enslavement lasted several centuries. During this time, there must have been some twenty generations of the invading creatures. Why is it that only their last generations proved incapable of adapting to local conditions?

"And, finally, why have none of our excavations for this period revealed any traces of the original masters of the planet? We find only rat skeletons. If we assume that the invaders annihilated the men, how can we explain not only their reappearance on the planet, but also their relatively speedy restoration of all they had lost?"

The workroom of the space station became silent, except for the heavy breathing of the Doctor and the tapping of the Commander's fingers on the arm of his chair.

"I would like to hear your opinion, Geologist."

The Geologist rose from his chair and went over to the two transparent sarcophagi that contained the results of the expedition's long and arduous labors. It had taken more than a year

169

of excavation, of scrupulous juxtaposition of thousands of find-
ings and careful analysis of the various hypotheses that sug-
geted themselves, in order to recreate the image of the former
inhabitants of the planet.

One of the sarcophagi contained a skillfully modeled full-
scale figure of a young man. Even according to terrestrial
standards, he was handsome, despite his lilac-colored skin and
his disproportionately large head. He was unquestionably a
product of an old, highly developed culture.

The other sarcophagus held a vile creature which had once
moved on two legs and was covered with gray shiny skin. Its
fat body, equipped with a pair of hands with extremely long
fingers, like the hands of a monkey, was crowned with a head
that resembled a rat's. The appearance of this rat-man was
frightening and revolting.

"I would like your opinion."

The Geologist gave an involuntary start at the sudden
recall to the present.

"Before I answer, I would like to ask the Doctor a question."

"Certainly."

"What makes you think that the rat-men are invaders from
space, and not natives of the planet?"

"They have an entirely different cell structure. They seem
to represent some sort of transitional stage between hydrocar-
bon protein structures and silico-organic ones. I have not been
able to find anything similar in the remains of the planet's
animal world. There were no other forms of this type on the
planet. Finally, you know very well that no rat-men were
found in any of our excavations for the period preceding the
era of decline."

The Geologist glanced at the sarcophagi again and
approached the Commander.

"I agree with the Doctor. Your theory explains nothing."

"Very well. Departure to Earth shall be postponed for six months. I will ask you to submit your plan for further work in two days. As of tomorrow, we shall reduce our rations."

The caterpillar jeep slowly made its way through lilac dust dunes. Millions of years ago there had been a city here. Now it was buried under layers upon layers of microscopic shells. Agile excavating machines were completing the work of clearing away deposits which had covered a large building made of pink stone.

The jeep turned the corner of the building and began a careful descent into a ditch, at the bottom of which stood a huge disc cast in a golden metal and set upon a pedestal. Was it a monument to astronauts? But the space ships of the masters of the planet looked quite different. All efforts to find on the planet even a trace of the metal of which the monument was made had proved fruitless. Could this huge structure be the handiwork of the rat-men? And what could be the meaning of the strange relief of alternating octahedrons and spheres on the pedestal? This motif had not been repeated on anything else uncovered by the excavations.

The Doctor's thoughts were interrupted by the grating of the caterpillar. The jeep had pitched sideways. The Doctor tried to open the door, but it was jammed against the foot of the monument.

They climbed out through the hatch in the roof of the jeep. The right caterpillar had sunk into a deep gap in the ground. A staircase, half buried in lilac dust, led into the darkness of an underground passage.

"I can't understand what's happening to the Doctor," said the Geologist, hammering down a case with minerals. "Why is he avoiding us?"

"He evidently feels guilty over the delay in our departure,

but he has no proof that he was right. We have wasted one hundred and twenty days. Now we must sacrifice all the exhibits we've gathered. The flight at this time will require much more fuel than it would have three months ago. We'll have to use the freight rocket fuel for the "Meteor." I can't forgive myself for giving in to your pressure so easily!"

"Perhaps we ought to speak to him again?"

"There's no point to it. If he insists on living alone in his laboratory, let him. He'll think better of it soon enough. Here he comes now. With an apology, if I am not mistaken."

The automatic doors of the space station opened softly and closed again behind the Doctor's back.

"You were right, Commander," he said with an embarrassed smile. "Everything was as you had thought. There was an invasion from space."

"I am delighted that you needed only a hundred and twenty days instead of the full six months to come to this conclusion. What was it that convinced you in the end?"

"Come to the monument. I'll show you everything."

"Here," said the Doctor, opening the armored doors of the underground hall. "This was once the site of one of the greatest battles in the universe, a battle to save the world's most ancient civilization. And here is what I have been able to reconstruct of the history of this battle."

Jumping around in a glass case was a small repulsive creature covered with shiny skin. Its fat body was crowned with a head resembling a rat's. It was a small copy of the figure in the sarcophagus, though it moved on four feet. Its glittering red eyes stared balefully at the three men.

"Where did you get this?"

The Commander's voice was hoarse.

"I brought it from Earth. Just a short while ago it was an ordinary guinea pig, until I infected it with a virus I found here."

172

The Doctor went to the table and pointed to one of the sealed glass retorts.

"The virus is shaped like an octahedron. I studied it most carefully. When it gets into an organism, it changes everything—the cell structure, the appearance, and, finally, the psychology of the host. It compels the organism to restructure itself according to the image coded in the chain of nucleic acids contained in this octahedron. Who knows from what depths of space this abomination found its way here? Now I must destroy the contents of these retorts, along with this little beast."

"So you believe the masters of this planet were simply stricken by disease?" asked the Geologist, his eyes fixed on the glass case.

"Unquestionably. It probably took no more than two generations before they were transformed into this type of rat-man."

"And who cured them?"

"Those to whom the monument was raised. Some unknown visitors from space. Here in the underground, hiding from the rat-men who had lost all vestiges of humanity, and risking infection every moment, they sought for the means of vanquishing the epidemic, and they succeeded. The spheres and octahedrons on the pedestal of the monument may be the symbol of the antivirus developed by them. Unfortunately, I have not been able to find any traces of it here."

"And what came next?"

"That we can only guess. Perhaps it happened as the Commander thinks. The inevitable aging of the planet may have led the rehumanized population to move to another part of the galaxy."

"I must apologize to you," said the Commander, holding out his hand to the Doctor. "I hope you will forgive me. And now, to work! We start back to Earth in three days."

His hand remained extended in the air.

"The start will be in two months, as agreed," said the Doctor, hiding his hand behind his back. "Two months of quarantine to make sure I have not caught this thing. And in the meantime no one must touch me."

THE TRAP

He hung, pressed by some monstrous weight, against the wall of the space ship. On his left, he saw the Geologist's foot and the Doctor's body, upside down.

We're like flies, he thought, trying to gather air into his lungs. Flies, squashed on the wall.

His broken ribs turned every breath into agony which almost made him lose consciousness. Very carefully he tried to breathe by moving only his diaphragm. He had to breathe in order not to faint, or he would not be able to think, and everything depended on that.

He had to understand what had happened.

He had known that something was going wrong for a long time, from the moment the instruments first registered that incomprehensible acceleration. In the beginning he had thought the ship was being deflected from its course by some powerful gravitational field, but the radio-telescope failed to reveal any accumulations of matter in this region of the cosmos.

Then the constellations had begun a game of leapfrog. They changed places, climbed on top of one another, turned blood-red or livid blue. Then came the sudden blow that had thrown him out of the pilot's chair, and this strange weight.

The ship was moving along a closed trajectory. He realized this the moment he regained consciousness.

Now he knew what was coming next.

He stared at the little pool of blood that had come out of the Doctor's mouth. Soon everything would start as in a film that was being run backward. This had happened over and over again. First the blood would flow back into the Doctor's tightly clenched lips. Then, with dizzying speed, tumbling head over heels, he himself would fly back into the pilot's chair, to be immediately thrown out of it again. He would strike the emergency instrument panel and then, with broken ribs and a crushed left hand, he would be thrown against the ship's wall. Then loss of consciousness, pain, and again an interval when it became possible to think about it all, until the sequences started again.

Time also moves along a closed circuit in this trap, he thought. An endless circle of time. Even Time cannot break out of here.

He came to again after striking the instrument panel. Again he had to conserve breath to keep his mind clear.

A whirlpool of Time and Space. This is the true meaning of hell: closed Space, where Time has caught itself by the tail; eternally repeating torture, and pale light, moving around a closed circuit: a world where everything turns in one spot, and only human thought seeks to breach the wall against which even Time is powerless.

He could not remember how many times the sequence of events had repeated itself. He watched the trickle of blood from the Doctor's mouth.

He is alive. Dead men don't bleed. His eyes are closed— that means he is unconscious. It's better for him. God knows what has happened to the Physicist. He was sitting on the couch. He'll probably be thrown back when the cycle starts again.

Again the headlong flight, the cracking bones, loss of consciousness—and desperate, probing thought.

The Time intervals are constantly shrinking. We have entered this trap and are going down a spiral. A little longer, and the craft will be caught in a sack where there is nothing but pale light. A sack where Time and Space are tangled into a tight knot, where eternity is indistinguishable from a single moment. Our engines are switched off, and our trajectory is determined by the accumulated quantity of movement and the curve of Space. Perhaps, if the engines are started, the spiral will begin to unwind. I must press the starting button on the emergency panel. But it's impossible. What can a fly do—a fly squashed on the wall?

With every curve of the spiral, the revolutions of Time increased in speed. Now there were only the briefest intervals when he was able to think. What he feared most of all was that his brain, exhausted by the repeating torture, would command his heart to stop.

Can a man die completely in a world where everything constantly keeps returning to its original state? I will be caught in an eternal succession of life and death, in ever accelerating tempo. What happens at the bottom of this sack? I must press the emergency button at the moment when I am thrown out of the chair. I must press it before my bones break, crashing against the panel.

Now he regained consciousness only when the trickle of blood had already disappeared into the Doctor's mouth.

I strike the control panel with my left side. The distance from my shoulder to the button is about twenty centimeters. If I hold out my elbow, it will strike the button.

After that everything merged into a continuous nightmare of headlong flights, the crashing of bones, pain, loss of consciousness, and stubborn efforts to find the right position for the elbow.

Chair, panel, wall, chair, panel, wall, chair, panel, wall. . . .

It seemed as if Time, gone berserk, was playing ball with man.

176

An eternity seemed to have passed before he felt the stab of intolerable pain in his left elbow.

He carried this pain through his unconsciousness like a dream of life.

Before he opened his eyes, he was aware of a blessed sense of weightlessness. Then he saw the face of the Doctor bending over him, and the familiar groups of constellations in the port. He wept, for he knew that he had conquered Time and Space.

The rest was done by the instruments. They took the ship back to its course and turned off the now unnecessary engines.

THE RETURN

The customary silence of the messroom was suddenly broken by the voice of the Geologist:

ISN'T IT TIME FOR US TO HAVE A TALK, COM-MANDER?

My heart's no damned good, the Commander told himself. It hammers like a boy's when he's caught in some mischief. Yet I have expected this conversation. But somehow I thought it would be started by the Doctor, not the Geologist. Strange that he sits there as though it didn't concern him at all. I detest his idiotic habit of tracing patterns on the tablecloth with his fork. Generally, he's gone pretty much to pot. Well, if the truth were told, we've all proved less than great. All, except the Physicist.

"YOU KNOW THAT I AM NOT A NOVICE IN SPACE FLIGHT . . ."

Yes, that is true. He has taken part in three expeditions. Uranium deposits on Venus, and something else along that line. The Doctor, too, has been on Mars twice. The chairman of the personnel committee had thought them both most suit-

177

able for the flight to Outer Space. They don't know a damned thing on those committees. A great thing—high plasticity of the nervous system! An ideal vestibular apparatus! Not worth a dime. I had no idea myself what Outer Space was like. Absolute, empty space. You fly for years at mad speed but in essence you hang in the same spot. Loss of all sense of time. Spatial hallucinations. The Doctor could write an excellent dissertation on cosmic psychoses. Yet everything was going so well at first, until the photon accelerator went to work.

The Physicist was, perhaps, the only one who did not feel a thing. He was too absorbed in his work. It's interesting that the Physicist was just the one they had not wanted to include in the expedition crew. Unstable blood pressure. The asses on those committees!

I KNOW THAT THE REGULATIONS OF THE COSMIC SERVICE FORBID CREW MEMBERS TO DISCUSS THE COMMANDER'S ACTIONS.

You're lucky you don't know the whole truth, or you'd say to hell with the regulations. The Physicist also spoke of the regulations before I killed him. I never thought I could do such a thing so calmly. Now I shall be tried. These two have already condemned me. Next comes the trial on Earth. I shall have to answer for everything: the failure of the expedition, the killing of the Physicist. It would be interesting to know if the statute of limitations still exists on Earth today. After all, according to terrestrial time at least a thousand years have passed since the Physicist died. A thousand years since we lost contact with Earth. For a thousand years we have hung in empty space, moving at a speed that's inconceivable to the human imagination. And in all this time, we have spent only several years in the rocket.

NEVERTHELESS, I SHALL PERMIT MYSELF TO BREAK THE REGULATIONS AND SAY WHAT I THINK.

178

We know neither our time, nor terrestrial time. Without knowledge of time it is impossible to do anything in Space. In order to determine the distance traversed it is necessary to integrate twice the acceleration with respect to time. We might have determined our speed by the Doppler effect but the spectrograph is ruined. How stupid it was to concentrate the most valuable equipment in the nose cone! Who would have thought the cobalt clock would let us down? We've always thought that the rate of radioactive decay is the most reliable measure of time. When the clock began those infernal tricks we were sure it had to do with the effect of speed on time. And then the cobalt indicator blew up, ruining everything in the nose section. The Physicist explained it all to me afterwards. It turned out that the quantity of charged particles in space exceeded the critical quantity by dozens of times. With the craft moving below the speed of light they created a powerful flow of hard radiation, causing a chain reaction in the radioactive cobalt. Almost simultaneously, the main reactor was automatically shut off. A chain reaction had begun there too. It was lucky the biological shield kept the radiation out of the cabin.

I KNOW THAT THE COSMOS BRINGS DISAPPOINTMENT TO THOSE WHO EXPECT TOO MUCH OF IT . . .

You and the Doctor have not yet experienced the most terrible disappointment of all. You still think you are returning to Earth. But how can I tell you that there is only one chance in a million that we shall return? I don't understand myself how I managed to get back to the solar system. Now I don't know my speed. Will the auxiliary reactors be powerful enough for deceleration? The best we can hope for is to come into stable orbit around the Sun. But for that I must know our speed. There is one chance in a million that we will succeed. If only the main reactor were functioning! Now it never will.

179

The Physicist transposed its rods. But this is something I cannot tell you. Loss of hope is the most terrible thing that can happen in space.

BUT THE WORST DISAPPOINTMENT I HAVE EXPERIENCED. . .

How many disappointments have I known? I was the first on Mars. The cold, lifeless desert immediately knocked out of my head all the youthful dreams of the blue-eyed beauties of distant worlds and the fantastic monsters with which I had hoped to enrich our zoological museums. I have never met anything in space that was remotely like the wonders of science fiction tales. Nothing but stunted lichens and yeast fungi. And the unsuccessful landing on Venus? Wasn't that full of disappointments and injured vanity? But then there were millions of people who sat all day and all night by their radio receivers, eagerly catching my every word; there were words of approval and encouragement from home, from Earth, and friends who came to my assistance. And now? The expedition is a failure. Even if there is a miracle and I succeed in bringing the ship back to Earth, what awaits me? Confession that I killed the Physicist and a few paltry facts about Outer Space which have long been known on Earth during the ten centuries since our departure. We'll look like cavemen who might have appeared in the twentieth century with the sensational news that you can make fire by rubbing together two pieces of wood. I don't know whether my reports have reached Earth. The only thing we have left now is the ruby transmitter, working on light frequencies. What is the good of its constant message: "Earth, Earth, this is the 'Meteor.' " Our receivers are not working. My reports are wandering somewhere in ether. Who remembers on Earth today that a certain 'Meteor' was sent into space a thousand years ago?

. . . IS THAT THE WAY TO THE COSMOS WAS

OPENED TO SUCH COWARDS AND MURDERERS AS YOU, COMMANDER.

I killed the Physicist. After the main reactor was shut off automatically, he sat down to make calculations. He came to me with two thick notebooks when the Geologist and the Doctor were asleep.

"We're in trouble, Commander," he said, sitting down on the sofa. "A chain reaction has started in the reactors, and the automatic controls have shut them off. We're caught in a vicious circle; until we reduce speed we cannot turn on the reactors. This flow of hard radiation which turned everything upside down is the result of our speed. We cannot reduce speed without starting the main reactor. I will have to shift the rods."

I knew what this meant.

"Very well," I said. "Give me the diagram and I will do it. You will be able to make the navigational calculations without me."

"You forget the regulations, Commander," he said, patting me on the shoulder. "Remember: Under no circumstances shall the Commander leave the cabin during flight."

"Nonsense!" I answered. "There are situations when—"

"Exactly. There are situations," he echoed. "I have not told you everything. After I change the position of the rods in the reactor, it will work only until you reduce speed sufficiently to eliminate the effect of hard radiation. After that it will go dead forever. I cannot tell you exactly at what speed this will happen. You will then be left only with the auxiliary reactors, which have no photon accelerators. I don't know what you will be able to do with them. Besides, you have no measure of time. Most of the automatic devices have been destroyed. Under these conditions, it is practically impossible to return to Earth. There may be one chance in a million, and this chance

181

lies in what is known as the astronaut's sixth sense. Do you understand now why you have no right to go into the reactor?"

Then we talked over the rest of it. We both knew that, having been in the reactor, he would not be able to return to the cabin. I was responsible for the lives of the Geologist and the Doctor. It would be madness to bring this lump of radiation into the cabin to die.

We agreed that I would destroy him with a jet of plasma.

"Excellent," he said, smiling. "At least, I will be able to see for myself that the reactor starts."

It seemed to me that he spent an eternity in that reactor. I saw him on the aft television screen when he had climbed out through the hatch. He smiled at me through the glass of his space suit and waved to indicate that everything was in order. I pressed the button.

When the Geologist and the Doctor asked where the Physicist was, I told them there had been an accident. I had sent him to check the photon accelerator and inadvertently switched on the reactor.

I could not tell them the truth. After that business with the trap, something had gone wrong with them. They must not know the hopelessness of our situation.

Then they stopped talking. Perhaps they spoke to one another when they were alone, but for several years I did not hear a word from them. For a thousand Earth years I heard no human speech. Then I noticed that they were fortifying themselves with the alcohol which was in the Doctor's keeping. When I took away the alcohol, the Doctor invented that devilish trick with the glass ball. Something along the line of Indian Yoga. They would stare at the glass ball until they lost all awareness. They went deeper and deeper into cosmic psychosis every day. I had to think of something. Then I gave them both a thrashing. I beat them until I saw fear in their eyes. Now, at least, I am able to make them exercise regularly and come to meals.

PERHAPS YOU WILL TRY TO GET RID OF US BEFORE RETURNING TO EARTH, AS YOU GOT RID OF THE PHYSICIST, BUT AT LEAST YOU WILL KNOW THAT WE HAVE SEEN THROUGH YOU, COMMANDER!

There is one chance in a million, but I must come out into a stable orbit, if only to try and save those two.

I WILL ANSWER FOR MY ACTIONS ON EARTH, said the Commander. AND NOW I ORDER YOU TO PUT ON YOUR ANTIBLACKOUT SUITS AND LIE DOWN. THE DECELERATION WILL BE VERY ABRUPT.

THE GRANDSON

They sat in the dining room, and I lay on the sofa in my grandfather's study and listened to their conversation.

Grandfather was telling them all sorts of wonderful stories.

I have a remarkable grandfather. All the boys envy me a little because I am his grandson. Everybody calls him the Old Astronaut. He was the first man on Mars, and he was the first to open the way into the Great Outer Space.

Now my grandfather is very old and cannot fly any longer, but all the young astronauts come to him for advice. He is the chief consultant of the Committee on Space Travel.

I love to watch grandfather's face. It is covered with scars and marks of burns. He lived through many adventures out there in the cosmos. A whole pile of books has been written about him, and we have them all.

I am terribly afraid that grandfather will die suddenly—he is so old.

My father is also out in space. Grandfather says that by the time he returns I'll be grown up. Papa doesn't know that mama died. Those who are out in space cannot be told bad news. Now I live with grandpa. He often tells me about the time when he was a young man and about the cosmos.

On grandfather's table there is a photograph of the crew of the "Meteor." They are all young there: grandpa, the Physicist, the Geologist, and the Doctor.

Grandpa loved the Physicist very much. When we go out for a walk, he always takes me to the Physicist's monument, on which is written:

FROM THE PEOPLE—TO THE HERO OF SPACE.

Grandfather loved the Geologist and the Doctor too. He says that at first they did not understand each other, but then they became close friends for the rest of their lives and made many space trips together. Now they are no longer alive.

Of all the friends that grandfather once had only the Designer and the Dispatcher are still living. They often visit us and speak about interesting things.

The other day they sat in the dining room, and grandfather was telling them how the "Meteor" was expected back on Earth in a thousand years, but it was caught in a trap where strange things happen with Time, and so they returned much sooner, when no one expected them. The Designer argued with him and said that such things do not happen to Time. Then grandfather told them about the Noneaters, and I lay on the sofa in the study and listened.

And then they left, and I started crying because I am still so little and cannot do anything.

Grandfather heard me crying and came to comfort me. He said that I would soon be big and fly into Outer Space, and that people will then be building space ships that will carry us faster than thought into the depths of the cosmos, and that I would discover new and marvelous worlds.

He tried to calm me down, but I cried and cried, because I

could not tell him that I love our own Earth more than anything in the world, and that I want to grow up as quickly as I can and do something wonderful on Earth.

I will be a doctor, and I will invent a way for people to live as long as they want to, and die only when they themselves decide to die.

THE NONEATERS

According to custom, we gathered on this day at the home of the Old Astronaut. Forty years ago we had signed his first mission to space, and although we remained on Earth, and he flew farther and farther out into the cosmos on every flight, thousands of common interests connected with our work had bound us in a friendship that grew stronger every year.

On this day we celebrated the fortieth anniversary of our first victory. As usual, we exchanged reminiscences and discussed plans. I will not conceal that the reminiscences grew longer every year, while the plans . . . However, I am digressing.

We had just concluded a heated debate about the paradoxes of Time and were still in that agitated frame of mind which persists after all the arguments are exhausted and every man remains with his original point of view.

"I am sure," said the Designer, "that Time flowing backward is just an invention of the mathematicians, just as the myth of the Noneaters is an invention of the astronauts. Both stories are equally unconvincing."

The familiar mocking lights flashed in the eyes of the Old Astronaut.

"You are mistaken," he said, filling our glasses again. "I saw the Noneaters myself. In fact, it was I who gave them this name. I can tell you how it happened."

185

THE OLD ASTRONAUT'S TALE

This was about thirty years ago. We were then flying on antediluvian annihilational engines which gave us no end of trouble. We were two parsecs away from Earth when we discovered that our photon accelerator required immediate repairs. The ship was going through a belt of intense radiation, and leaving the cabin, which was equipped with a reliable biological shield, was out of the question.

The only salvation would be landing on a planet possessing a sufficiently dense atmosphere. Fortunately, this opportunity soon presented itself. Our radio-telescope found a small system directly in our course, consisting of a central luminary and two planets. Our instruments recorded the presence of an atmosphere containing oxygen on one of these planets.

Now we were prompted not only by the need to repair the damage but also by the excitement of explorers, which is familiar to all who had ever discovered in the cosmos conditions suitable for the emergence of life.

You know our little old ships. The youngsters today consider them simply funny but I recall them with regret. They had none of the comforts of the present liners, and their crews were ridiculously small, but I think they were invaluable in cosmic reconnaissance. They did not require cosmic landing stations and, most importantly, they were easily convertible to jet planes of excellent maneuverability.

Our crew consisted of the Geologist, the Doctor, and myself, in the capacity of commander, pilot, and mechanic. The fourth member of the crew was my old space companion—the dog Ruslan.

We could barely contain our impatience when clouds flickered across the television screen, hiding the surface of the mysterious planet. We knew a little about it already. Its mass was much like the Earth's, and the period of its revolution

186

around the central luminary was equal to the time of its revolution around its own axis. Thus, like our moon, it was always turned to its sun with only one side. Its atmosphere consisted of twenty per cent oxygen, seventy per cent nitrogen, and ten per cent argon. Such an atmosphere would make it unnecessary for us to work in our space suits.

Each of us busily conjectured about the appearance and character of the masters of our future haven. Unfortunately, we were quickly disappointed. Our ship flew three times around the planet at a low altitude but there was nothing to indicate the presence of living beings on it. The bright side of the planet was a parched desert, and the opposite side—a solid glacier. Even the zone of constant twilight along their boundaries was devoid of any vegetation. The lack of vegetation despite the presence of oxygen in the atmosphere remained a puzzle.

Finally, we chose a landing site in a region with the most moderate climate. The damage in the accelerator turned out to be trifling, and we hoped to continue our journey after several days, according to the terrestrial calendar.

While we were making the repairs, we also continued our study of the planet. Its soil consisted of basalts with considerable accumulations of manganese oxides. The presence of oxygen in the atmosphere was evidently due to the processes of reduction of these oxides.

Neither our tests of atmospheric samples, nor our analyses of the water of the hot and cold springs, which abounded on the planet, showed anything that might indicate the presence of even the most primitive forms of life. The planet was hopelessly dead.

Everything was ready for our departure when something happened that changed our plans. We were working on the launching platform when we heard Ruslan barking furiously. It must be said that Ruslan was a dog of wide experience, and

only something entirely extraordinary could have made him
bark. However, even I had to exclaim in surprise at what we
saw.

A strange procession was moving toward a wide brook that
flowed some fifty meters from our ship. At first I thought they
were penguins. The same imperturbable calm, the same digni-
fied bearing, the same hobbling gait that we find in the deni-
zens of our antarctic coast. But this was only a first impression. The creatures filing past us resembled neither penguins
nor anything else known to man.

Imagine an animal about as tall as a kangaroo walking on
its hind legs. At the side of the body they had tiny three-
fingered projections. Their small heads had two eyes and were
adorned with a crest similar to a rooster's comb. A long thin
tube dangled beneath a single nasal aperture. But the most
remarkable feature these beings possessed was a completely
transparent skin, through which could be seen a bright-green
circulatory system.

When the procession caught sight of us, it stopped. Ruslan
ran around the strangers with loud barking but his barking
seemed to produce no impression at all. For a while they studied us with large blue eyes. Then, as though at a command,
they turned and walked to another brook nearby. Evidently,
we had simply ceased to interest them. They dropped to their
knees, lowered their tubes into the water, and remained motionless for a good half-hour.

All this was in direct contradiction to our conclusion that
the planet was uninhabited. These beings could not have been
its only inhabitants, even if only because, like all animals, they
required organic food. Everything alive that I had ever seen in
space existed within a single biological complex, assuring the
vital activities of all its components. Outside of such symbiosis, in the broadest sense of the word, no forms of life are
possible. Had we simply overlooked this whole complex?

I cannot say that these ideas, which flashed through my mind while I observed the inhabitants of the planet, were particularly pleasant. As commander of the expedition, I was not only responsible for the flight, but also for the correctness of the scientific information returned to Earth. Departure was now out of the question. The start had to be postponed until we solved this new riddle.

Having quenched their thirst, the mysterious creatures sat down in a circle. What they did reminded me of a singers' contest I had once seen in Central Asia. Each of them took his turn to move into the middle of the circle. The colorless comb on his head would begin to flash with varicolored lights. The rest watched this play of colors in utter silence. After completing the full program, they rose to their feet and set off single file on the return march. We followed them.

I shall not weary you with a description of all our attempts to arrive at some conception of the life of these creatures. We spent more than two months watching them.

They lived on the bright side of the planet. It is difficult to say how they spent their time. They simply did nothing. For about two hundred hours they lay under the burning rays of their sun, until it was time to go to the brook to drink. At the brook, they invariably repeated the scene we had observed the first time.

They reproduced by gemmation. After the offspring grew up on the back of the adult, the parent died. Thus, their number on the planet always remained constant. They had no diseases, and throughout our stay we never observed a premature death.

We were especially struck by one of their peculiarities: they did not eat. This was why I gave them the name of Noneaters.

We dissected several dead Noneaters, and found nothing in them resembling digestive organs. How, then, did their metabolic processes take place? They could not, after all, live merely on water.

The Doctor studied their metabolism by testing several living individuals. They were obviously displeased, but submitted unprotestingly to his taking of blood samples, and allowed masks to be put over their faces during gas analysis. It seemed that they were simply too lazy to resist.

We were already beginning to lose patience. Our calculations showed that further postponement of the start of our return trip to Earth would result in unfavorable flight conditions, connected with large expenditures of fuel, which we had in short supply, but none of us was willing to give up hope of solving this new secret of life.

At last the long-awaited day came when the Doctor succeeded in coordinating all his data, and the Noneaters ceased to be a riddle to us. We concluded that the Noneaters were not complete and unified organisms. In their blood there were bacteria which utilized the light of their sun in the process of breaking down carbon dioxide and synthesizing nutritive substances from atmospheric nitrogen, carbon and water vapor, which they then supplied to the organism of the Noneaters. The processes of photosynthesis were facilitated by the transparent skin of these remarkable animals. The multiplication of the bacteria in the bodies of the Noneaters took place only in a mildly alkaline medium. As soon as there were too many bacteria, the endocrine glands of the Noneaters produced hormones that raised the acidity of the blood, thus regulating the concentration of nutritive substances in the organism. It was an astonishing example of symbiosis, hitherto unknown to science.

I must confess that the Doctor's discovery made me ponder a good deal. No living creature in the cosmos has been given so much by nature as the Noneaters. They were spared the necessity to obtain food, or to care for their progeny; they were not threatened by overpopulation, they did not know anything about the struggle for existence, and they were never sick. It would seem that nature had done everything to assure the high intellectual development of these creatures. And yet they were not too different from my dog Ruslan. They had no society of any kind. Each individual lived entirely on his own, without communication with others of his kind, save the apparently meaningless games with the flashing combs by the brook.

Frankly speaking, I began to feel a kind of revulsion against these darlings of nature, and left their strange planet without regrets.

"And you never returned?"

"By chance, I was there again ten years later, and was more astonished by what I saw this time than I had been by the Doctor's original discovery. On my second visit, I found the rudimentary beginnings of social relations among the Noneaters, and even a sort of social industry."

"And what prompted this development?" asked the Designer with some skepticism.

"Fleas."

There was the sound of breaking glass. The Designer looked down regretfully at his trousers, stained with wine.

"I am very sorry," he said, gathering the splinters from the floor. "I think this was your favorite wine glass, but your joke was so unexpected . . ."

"I had no intention of joking," the Old Astronaut interrupted him. "Everything was exactly as I say. We had been so certain that no life existed on the planet that we failed to take the usual measures for decontamination. Evidently, a few of Ruslan's fleas had made themselves at home with the Noneaters and prospered there. I've told you that the Noneaters have very short upper extremities. If they did not scratch each other's backs and unite in the effort to catch the fleas, they would simply have been eaten alive.

"I don't know which of the Noneaters was the first to discover that manganese peroxide is an excellent remedy against fleas. In any case, I saw a factory producing this powder. They had even managed to invent some sort of a primitive mill for milling it."

We were silent for a while. Then the Designer said:

"Well, I must go now. The twelfth extragalactic expedition is starting out tomorrow. I am invited to the celebration. I suppose you will be there too?"

We left together.

"Ah, those cosmic stories!" he sighed, as we entered the elevator.